Mack Book

By

Gill Burnett

Other Books by Gill Burnett

Take Note
Note Taken
Last Note

Cushie Butterfield
Who Said That???
Show Me a Sign!!

By Gill Burnett & Freddie Jones

Eddie the Elf

(1) RETURN OF THE MACK #markmorrison

Mack stumbled into car sales!
Since leaving 6th form he had spent his days working in a Call Centre; he had never thought it was his 'calling'. But it paid well and if he was honest it was a very female orientated workplace and it played to his ego! He had been there way too long; but he was lazy and physically looking for a new job just filled him with dread. But he was also very bored; there was little room for promotion without having to go and get additional qualifications which realistically would only give him an extra quid an hour. Even the endless supply of new staff who had once put a spring in his step and an extra dab of aftershave every morning; now had lost their appeal.

And it was because of one of the new staff members that he ended up hiding in the gent's toilets scrolling through his Facebook and spotted a little advertisement for a car salesman at a local garage.

WANTED
Car Sales Executive
For Local Family Run Garage
Experience Preferred but not Essential
Company Car and Excellent Renumeration Package
Call/Message
L Pearson

It was one of those adverts on Facebook that if you didn't see it first time around and no one Tagged you in then it was lost to you forever! He had no experience in cars; he had one and that was one of the reasons the job appealed to him. His Car! Or to put it more correctly; his Nan's old car! When he had passed his test when he was 17; his Granddad,

God Bless him had given Mack the little old car he had kept and loved in his garage for 5 years since his Nan had died.

Mack was over the moon. When he had taken the driving lessons that his mam had saved up so hard to get him for his 17th birthday he had never dreamt that he would be able to have a car of his own. All the way through his lessons he had assumed that he would share his mam's old Astra and in his imagination, he could see the arguments that those arrangement would make! But there it was, parked on the drive when he got back home on the day of his test with his Mam and Granddad standing proudly next to it! Mack actually cried. He didn't even know that his Granddad had kept the car; but he had and it was pristine! Very different to how it looked now in the works car park! Mack actually felt embarrassed that he had let it fall into such bad disarray and nowadays only used it when he had to and literally hide it when he knew he was seeing his Granddad!

It had got so bad with the car recently; if he planned to go anywhere where he knew he would be seen by anyone he knew; he got a taxi! It surprised him that it made it through it's MOT; luckily one of his best mates was a mechanic and every year Mack handed Josh the car a couple of weeks before the MOT was due for him to get it into some sort of shape; every year his Credit Card took a bigger and bigger hit! But it got him backwards and forwards to work and he would always be grateful to his Granddad for giving him the car in the first place. And if that car could speak if would have some stories to tell! It would make his Granddad's toes curl; or would it; he hadn't always been 76 and if the old photographs were anything to go by; Mack had inherited his good looks from his Granddad!

But the car really did need to go! Another MOT loomed on the horizon and this year the balance owed on his Credit Card far outweighed the money available!

He was crap with money! There was always somewhere to go or something he really needed to buy so never quite managed to save any money up! His wages went into his bank on the last day of the month and you could bet your life on it by the 10th at the latest he was having to borrow money off his mam. Mack was back living with his mam; he had moved in with his girlfriend when he was 19 but 6 months ago had gone back to his mam with his tail between his legs with a reassurance that she had been right all of the time and he was nowhere near ready to settle down. The situation wasn't ideal; his mam had got herself a boyfriend since Mack had moved out; their relationship was a lot more serious than Mack had thought when he had asked his mam if he could move back! He was happy she was happy though and spent as much time as he could out of the house. And that was the reason that he had been spending his lunch break hiding in the gent's toilets!

Melissa! She had only been working at the Call Centre a few weeks when she tagged along to Friday Night Drinks! It was one of those silly customs that people who work all day together do. They leave work on a Friday night and head straight for the pub to spend even more time together! It was usually a mixed bag of people and every week there was a different crowd; there was only Mack and a couple of others who managed to make it there every week; Mack usually because Friday night tended to be date night for his Mam and Tom and he really didn't want to cramp their style by being the third wheel. So the Friday Night Ritual kept him out of the house until way after 11 when all at home was quiet and still.

(2)   OOPS I DID IT AGAIN!   #britneyspears

But to be honest most Fridays he never made it home. There was always somewhere else he could be. Melissa was somewhere else he could be! He knew she liked him even before they got to the pub; he just knew these things. Most women did! He was funny and charming and because his mam had brought him up on her own, she had always instilled in him that he should complement women on how they looked. And he did. No one in the Call Centre escaped the Mack Attack no matter who they were or how they looked. It was nice to be nice and he liked the effect a nice word had on women!

The drinks had flowed the Friday before; it was still the beginning of the month, so Mack's contactless card was pinging along nicely and the conversation had turned who wanted to move on after the next drink! As everyone hadn't long been paid; there was a fair old few moving on to a livelier bar and new girl Melissa was included.

A few hours later Mack found himself sneaking up Melissa's parents' house stairs and into her bed! She was nice; she had been sweet and funny in the pub and when she dragged him on to the dance floor and he saw her moves, it was a done deal; he wanted her! And that's exactly what he got as he lay on her bed with her bouncing up and down on him he struggled to focus on her face. He had drank quite a bit and to be honest he had been in this situation many times before; so when the moment of release came he truly didn't know who he was with! It wasn't a feeling he liked and to make up for the fact he had forgot her; he spent as long as he could in full Mack Attack mode and made sure she had a night she wouldn't forget, even if he would.

The weirdest thing he always felt after a night like the one with Melissa was waking the next morning. He woke that morning before she did; he had a raging thirst and was desperate for a drink; but in the early morning light it took a few minutes to realise where he was; he wasn't at home in his own bed; or in bed he had shared with Carly for the past few years; he was in Melissa from the office's bedroom and looking around; he knew he had made a mistake!

As pretty and sweet and funny as she was; she was young; looking around her room she was probably younger than he had first thought. She was by no means a virgin; she knew what she was doing; but mixed around the room with her clothes and make-up were teddy bears and trophies. From what he could make out from the silhouette of them in the early morning light; it looked like she was a dancer in her even younger days! Somehow, in his hung over brain and in the pit of his stomach; he knew that she didn't expect to be a one-night stand; this girl would expect more!

Even as he woke her to let him out of the house; he felt like the biggest shit when she beamed a massive smile at him and offered to make him a coffee; which against his better judgement he accepted and then lay in her bed kicking himself as she left to go and make it! She mustn't have had as much to drink as him because she was as fresh as a daisy and didn't think twice about jumping into a car with her when she offered to drive him home. They must have exchanged numbers the night before because as he kissed her before he got out of the car, she said she would text him later.

And boy was she as good as her word. He had barely got home, showered and changed when the first text came through.

    Mel   - had a grt nght thanks

Obliged to text back, after all he would see her at work on Monday he replied
    Me   - me too x

And from then on it was relentless. Did he fancy meeting up later? Did he want to go to the beach the next day? On and on it went! He was polite and replied. He didn't want her to feel crap; but he also knew without a shadow of doubt; she wasn't for him and if he saw her again, she would totally get the wrong idea! So, he kept busy the whole weekend; even when he hadn't had plans he made sure he had some! He felt like a complete twat! It had happened in the past; but not with people he worked with. If he slept with someone at work, he made sure they knew the rules of the game; it was sex!

(3) MANIC MONDAY   #thebangles

He had slept with quite a few of his workmates, sometimes more than once; in fact it was a dalliance with a work-mate that had put an end to his relationship with Carly; but the girls had been older and didn't seem to mind when Mack didn't call or text! The funny thing was though, he was friends with them all and they were all friends with each other in some shape or form. He sometimes wondered if they talked about him and his performance! It made him a little bit uncomfortable, but they all went out of their way to still communicate with him, he had even been to a wedding of one of 'his girls' and the christening of another's baby! He had taken some stick for that one seeing as the baby boy had a stock of dark hair just like his; but Nikki had been not long after he had started working there and unless she had been an elephant; that baby certainly wasn't anything to him!

So, the job opportunity seemed like a sign from God that Monday lunchtime. He had kept Melissa at arm's length all weekend and he had been overly friendly with her when he got to work; but he knew whatever he did or said next to her would hurt her or at the very least damage her ego and he didn't want to do either. He just wanted it to be forgotten about!

He sent a message to the garage. He said he was very interested in the vacancy they had; that he could send them a CV and that he was available for interview at their request. It seemed like a bizarre way to apply for a job; when he had applied for the Call Centre there had been forms and an aptitude test; followed by face to face interviews; short list; more tests and then two more interviews! To just send a message seemed sloppy even to him. But he did it and off it went and as he made his way out of the Gents and back to his desk for his afternoon shift; he didn't hold out much hope!

With his mobile tucked away in his drawer for the next few hours until his next break; for once he concentrated on work and put thoughts of Melissa out of his head. Making his way to the vending machine for a drink at break-time he glanced at his phone; there were a few messages and his heart slumped; Melissa, from somewhere in the building must have managed to use her mobile even when there were consequences off the team leaders when staff were caught with them. He didn't even bother opening the messages; just slid the phone back into the drawer and decided he would deal with them after he finished work!

But Mack was wrong. There was only one message from Melissa; just hoping he was having a good Monday. The rest of the messages were off mates and there was one from Len Pearson Cars; he kicked himself for having missed it! Thinking it was a standard thank you for your interest but no thank you; he was pleasantly surprised when the message read that they would like to know more about him and would he be interested in going in to see them for a chat. He couldn't believe it!

Sitting in his car he sent a message back saying he would love to come in but was at work until 6pm all week! Before he even got home his phone flashed up with a message; it took all his resolve not to pull over and read it, but he held off until he was parked up at home. Yes they said, that would be fine; would Thursday be convenient about 7??

Of course it would be convenient; he messaged back saying he would be there Thursday and looked forward to meeting him. It was the best news he had got in a long time; he might not know much about selling cars, but he was no mug and he could learn. He spent the rest of the week researching all about Len Pearson Cars; he even went to the pictures with Melissa on the night before the interview; somehow knowing there may be a chance of moving on, it didn't seem so daunting spending some time with a nice, pretty, funny girl. He didn't tell anyone about the interview; it was so far away from what he did for a living he didn't want to end up with egg on his face, so he kept stum!

He was actually a bag of nerves at work the day of his interview; he couldn't remember a time when he had felt like it before. Every call he took was a pain in the neck and the hands on the clock seemed to tick by slower than normal. But eventually clocking off time arrived and he dived out of the office; into his car and straight into his gym with washbag and suit in hand.

Twenty minutes later he was back in the car and speeding; well tootling towards Len Pearson Cars and whatever the future had in store for him.

(4) INTERVIEW   #robbiewilliams

Mack did two drive pasts the garage; even in his old jalopy it had got him there faster than he thought and he was far too early; at least ten minutes for a respectable ten minutes early for an appointment. So he drove past a couple of times trying to take in what he could see in first impressions.

The first thing he noticed was it was old school. The pitch was festooned in bunting; he loved it. Somewhere in his memory he could remember sitting watching some old television series with his Nan and Granddad, but for the life of him he couldn't remember what it was called! It gave him a little shiver; de ja vue?? He wasn't sure, he just knew something stirred in him; hopefully it was a good feeling!

Not wanting to be seen getting out of his own car; he parked a couple of streets away and sent up a silent apology to his Nan and Granddad. He wasn't so much ashamed of it, it was just; well you know!!!

By the time he walked to the garage the bright lights that had lit up the pitch were switched off; only the lights from what Mack assumed was the office block could be seen. There was no one around and as he made his way towards the door; he soaked in the cars he passed. It was like a box of Quality Street; there seemed to be something for everyone. The were Corsas and Fiestas; a Focus and an Astra and they were just the ones he noticed; but parked near the doorway was his ultimate vehicle; it was a top of the range crew cab with lots of shiny chrome; it took all of his resolve not to go over and have a closer look. But if he didn't get the job it was certainly out of his price range so why make himself even more miserable he thought to himself as he made his way into the building.

Not sure what to do or where to go he sat down in the waiting area and waited for someone to put in an appearance. Thinking there may be some kind of test; he tried to take in his surroundings; there were pictures of classic cars everywhere. Lots of them looked like they had been photographed on the pitch outside; there was the familiar bunting in the background; but surely all these cars were long gone now. He was so absorbed that he didn't hear the door opening and a young woman come and stand next to him!

'Can I help you? She asked him giving him a look up and down! If he said so himself; a suit suited him! I'm Mack I'm here to meet L Pearson,' That's me Mack, do you want to come this way?' Following behind her; he tried to keep his mind on the fact that he was here for an interview and not chasing skirt; but what a swing she had and as they made their way along a short corridor; he could only think how unexpectedly fit L Pearson was!

Ushering him into an office she asked him to take a seat and sat herself down in the chair opposite! The scenario he had played out in his head about how the interview would go was nowhere near the reality he was in now! Trying to regain some composure he fished in his pocket for his CV; something he had hastily pulled together that morning on the off chance they asked for it! Smiling she took it off him and spent the next few minutes reading through it before placing it on the desk in front of her!

(5)   GETTING TO KNOW YOU   #julieandrews

'So do you want to tell me a bit about yourself?' She asked relaxing back in the chair to listen; she had a pen in her hand and as Mack set of with his monologue of his greatest achievements and what an asset, he thought he would be to her; she leaned forward and seemed to be scribbling on his CV!

She really is quite a looker; Mack thought to himself as he tried to dredge through everything he had done with his life since school; career wise that was. As he talked, he began to regain some of his composure. He couldn't get over the fact that he had been expecting to be getting interviewed off a man! All the research he had done had indicated that L Pearson was the owner of the company, and he was the man in many of the photographs on their website; he could bet his life on it not seeing this version of L Pearson, he would have remembered her! But he kicked himself that he hadn't looked into the infrastructure of the company properly; he was at a disadvantage, and it was of his own doing!

She asked him about why he thought he was the right candidate for the job. He responded with as clear and concise answers as he could; he may not have any car sales experience but that wasn't necessarily a bad thing; he would be coming with no preconceptions, and they would be able to train him to their own high standards; he was a blank canvas for them! He may have been mistaken; but Mack thought he saw something of a flicker of agreement as she listened to what he had to say about himself!

The questions went on and on; all the time the woman scribbled on his freshly printed CV. As she made notes he had chance to have a good look at her. She was difficult to age; maybe mid-thirties, very young to be running a business the size of L Pearson; especially with it being the type of business it was; from all accounts it was still very much a male dominated world; the used car sales business!

She asked him about himself; what he did for fun so on and so forth. From the way she said it he had been on his social media accounts; that was the thing about today's world; everything was out there for everyone to see. So, if she had been doing her own research on him; she would have a fair idea what type of lad Mack was!

After he had finished telling her about his love of football and the gym and spending time with his friends; she surprised him by asking him if he wanted a coffee. Saying he would love one; he was left to his own devices for a few minutes, which gave him chance to evaluate how the interview was going! He didn't think he had come across as a moron; but he certainly hadn't come across of someone who would be an asset to her company! It was all going to hinge on what exactly they wanted and how he conducted himself over the next few minutes!

(6)   KILLER QUEEN   #queen

He glanced at his watch and was surprised to see that 45 minutes had passed. While he continued to wait for L Pearson to come back; he looked around the office. It certainly didn't look like a woman's office. There were no tell-tale signs like that of the female Team Leaders at the Call Centre; no little nick-knacks strewn across the desk; or 'Dreamboy' calendars hanging on the wall. He was about to stand up and have a good look around when the door opened, and she was back; with two streaming mugs of coffee in her hand. The mugs weren't the only things steaming; so was she!! If she had seen the look on his face as she placed his coffee in front of him; she didn't show it, but it would be an everyday occurrence for her, Mack thought to himself.

Sitting there, the interview seemed to be over. She asked about which gym he went to; where he went to in town etc; he felt like he was sitting talking to one of the girls at the office! And before he knew it, he was in Mack Attack mode; he didn't know how it had happened; but somehow the coffee break seemed to break down the barriers and they both seemed to forget the reason they were there and chatted and flirted while they drank their drinks.

When she asked about wives and girlfriends and kids, he knew he was on rocky ground. He should have told her about Melissa he thought afterwards, that would have settled the situation down. But in the heat of the moment, he said he was happily single; even added that there were far too many types of sweets in the sweetshop to be stuck with one brand. What the hell!

The banter went on for a few minutes; the more they chatted the more he could see the woman in her emerging and the boss ebbing away. When she stood up and went to the door and turned the key; he wasn't surprised. When she came to him and turned his chair to face her; he wasn't surprised. When she lifted her dress and straddled herself across his knee; again, he wasn't surprised!

Just as he went in to kiss her, she said 'so how much do you want this job then Mack?' Images of a casting couch flew through his mind. If she wanted a performance that was what she was going to get. 'I'll show you Miss Pearson!' he muttered before crushing his mouth down on hers!

Later as he tidied the desk, and she went to unlock the door; he smiled. She had been as good as she looked. He had no idea what was happening about the job, he couldn't really expect to be in with a chance now. He felt like an idiot and not an idiot at the same time; but as he got ready to leave, idiot idiot was far out-weighing anything else.

The door had no sooner been unlocked when an older man came bursting through; it gave Mack a scare; was this Miss Pearson's husband come to catch her out??

'Mack, Mack, I am so sorry; there were temporary roadworks on the A1 and I got stuck coming back from the Auctions, I didn't have your number to call you to postpone the interview but luckily, I managed to get hold of Eleanor. I'll grab myself a coffee and then we'll talk!'

The man leant over to grab Mack's hand! 'I'm Len Pearson for my sins and of course you have met my daughter Elle.......'

(7) NO REGRETS   #robbiewilliams

The second interview was very different from the first. Len Pearson knew his salt and Mack was being put through the ringer; he had obviously interviewed many times before and knew how to get what he wanted with minimum palaver!

As Mack answered question after question all he could think about what he had done! Realistically Elle Pearson had used him; making him think that she was The L Pearson had been a low blow; the only thing she had to gain was a sex! But then he was as guilty as she was; he should have kept it professional; he could have stopped it at any time but he hadn't. He had no one to blame but himself and his inability to walk away from a pretty face.

By the time the interview was over he was worn out. Len Pearson walked him out, promising to contact him in a day or two! By all accounts the interview had gone well, but Mack wasn't hopeful. Mack waited while Mr Pearson secured the pitch and locked it for the night; it was the least he could do; it was almost 9 o'clock. Shaking hands; they parted ways and Mack headed off towards his car; with a toot and vroom, Len Pearson headed off into the darkness in his Jaguar. The one that got away a despondent Mack thought to himself as he fumbled for his keys in his suit pocket.

The saving Grace was that he hadn't told anyone he was even being interviewed for another job; all he could do was put it down to experience and if something like that ever came up again; he would be willing, ready and able! But for the interview not for wasting his attention and energy on an interloper – even if they were as hot as Elle Pearson.

And then it was Friday and for once he was miserable. He spent the whole day kicking himself; he had been led by his dick just like he had been too many times before! Looking back he had been given a great opportunity, neither Elle or Len had mentioned they had been or were intending to interview anyone else. He thought he had been in the right place at the right time for once in his life; but he had been in the right place at the wrong time; if only fate had stepped in and he had a reason to be late and had called ahead to tell them of his delay; surely then he would have known that Len Pearson was running late himself and it would have been well!

But it was done now; and as his workday ended, he found himself following everyone else into the pub. This week he knew his contactless card wouldn't hold out and once the cash in his pocket had run out, he would have to make his way slowly home and hang around outside until the coast was clear and he could safely go in without disturbing his mam and Tom or worse catch them being overly cosy with each other.

Melissa was part of the group; he had the feeling everyone knew how intimate they had been since the last time they were there. It didn't matter! It wasn't the first time he had been in that position; to be honest Melissa had probably achieved more than others; they were still texting and he had been to the flicks with her; but even sitting opposite her all blonde curls and smiles; he knew she was only ever going to be friend material. If she was going to be anything else he truly wouldn't have been so willing to show Elle Pearson how much he wanted the job would he?

By closing time his pockets were empty and he was jumping into the waiting taxi and heading home with Melissa. Nowhere near as drunk as the week before; he was relieved when Melissa said her mam and dad were away for the weekend and they would have the place to themselves! He just couldn't not. He had been annoyed and disappointed in himself all day and the thought of someone distracting him and making him feel better for a little while was just too good an offer to turn down!

Mack knew he shouldn't take advantage of Melissa; she really was one of the good ones! She was a natural; he remembered vividly that when he saw her the previous Saturday morning, she had looked as good as she had the night before, something that was a rare occurrence for him. The number of times he had pulled a 'worldie' the night before only to wake up next to a girl who resembled little of her night-time alter ego. He didn't want to lead Melissa up the garden path; he still thought that she was friend material; but maybe she could be a friend with benefits! He liked her. She was funny and kind; when she realised that Mack didn't have much money on him, she got him drinks when she got hers! She didn't make a big fuss, just put the drink down in front of him and smiled.

He liked being in her company; with the house being empty there wasn't the frantic rush to the bedroom. When she suggested cheese on toast for supper; he actually kissed her. He hadn't had cheese on toast for supper since he had lived with Carly, it had been their thing; a little pang of sadness shot through his body, he hadn't really thought about her for months, it had ended badly and of course it was his fault. Thinking about it still made him feel crap! He would probably always feel a shit about how it had all ended.

But for the now there was Melissa and her cheese on toast. His issues with Carly could wait and by the time the cheese on toast was eaten and Melissa was on her knees making him feel better; Carly and their cosy suppers were forgotten.

(8)   DON'T LOOK BACK IN ANGER   #oasis

The rest of the weekend was mainly spent at home. He hadn't got back from Melissa's until lunchtime and by the time he got himself sorted and collected his car from work, it was teatime and he couldn't be bothered to go and meet up with his mates.

He was in a strange, morose kind of mood, something he didn't experience very often. Still upset with himself for throwing away a great opportunity; in his mind he thought his interview with Elle had gone really well up until the coffee break and he had the job in the bag, but maybe that was what they called looking back at things through rose tinted spectacles. Maybe he had done a shit job and her dad would never have given him a job in a million years and that's why she had taken the opportunity to dance the tango with him knowing for certain that she was never going to see him again.

Then there was Melissa. She really was a sweet girl and the night he had spent with her had been amazing, but she wasn't for him, not long term. He needed more! He instinctively knew with women whether they had that something about them that would keep him interested. He had slept with Melissa again because she had been there and he needed some comfort, he doubted that they would be getting it on again; he just needed to make her realise that they would be better off as friends. It would have been easy if he had got the new job, he would have left the Call Centre and settled things down by saying he had to use all his energy on his new job and didn't need any distractions; even a distraction as pretty as her. But now what?

The cheese on toast had unsettled him too. He hadn't spoken to Carly for months, but the urge to pick up his mobile and call her was strong. He didn't want to see her or get back or anything; he just wanted to say he was sorry and none of it was her doing. He wanted to tell her that he was just a dick; who literally couldn't keep it in his pants. She hadn't done anything wrong. He wouldn't though. The truth of it was he didn't want to try and call her in case she had blocked his number. Somehow the thought of Carly not wanting him in her life made him sad; if she didn't, he really didn't want to know! He had really thought that he had found what he had been looking for with Carly, obviously not!

He slept badly, he just couldn't find a spot and spent most of the night tossing and turning. When he eventually fell asleep his sleep was filled with mad nightmares which woke him in a cold sweat. The sound of his mobile ringing started pulling him out of the deep sleep he had eventually fallen in to. He ignored it, it would just be one of his mates wanting a lift or something. The phone tinged and he knew a voicemail had been left. He fell back to sleep and when he eventually woke he could smell roast beef and knew he had slept way beyond his usual Sunday morning.

Mack was still feeling a bit off. He had nowhere to be in particular so lay in bed and once again played a repeat on what happened at Len Pearson Cars. As much as he knew he had blown it; Elle Pearson stirred something in his boxer shorts and he spent the next few minutes remembering how she looked and tasted and felt. She was definitely one of those women that would literally keep his pecker up! She was unbelievably hot!

(9)   WE ARE FAMILY   #sistersledge

Not until he had finished in the shower and got dressed did, he think about checking his mobile. Picking it up he ignored the messages and clicked on to Facebook, no Eleanor Pearson that he recognised so he tried Elle Pearson and there she was, smiling back just as he had remembered her. But that was all he could see; her privacy settings only allowed him to see a couple more pictures and in those ones she was with a group of people and he could barely see her. He thought of sending her a friend request then thought better of it.

Flicking on to his own friend list he searched out Carly. She hadn't blocked him on Facebook so that made him a bit better, clicking on to her profile he was surprised when he saw a picture of her with a man. Mack didn't recognise him, but they looked happy together. A little pain shot across his heart, and he selfishly thought, well they are still in the honeymoon period when everyone is happy, but it won't last. The bloke was punching well beyond his weight, but then he instantly felt bad. She so deserved to be happy! He continued to scroll through her Facebook and to all accounts; Carly and Liam had been together for a few months.

They were in a relationship on Facebook so it must be real. Continuing down through her posts and pictures he was wasn't shocked to find that there wasn't one single photograph of Carly and him.

Photographs he knew he had been in with Carly had been cropped to remove him. It was like they had never existed. Three years of happy memories had disappeared! It was a gut-wrenching realisation. They really had been mostly happy! Mack had been faithful to her for a long time; much longer than he had been faithful to anyone before. But about a year into their relationship, when they had been living together for about 3 months, he shit on her; he had got away with it and because he had got away scot free, he did it again and again and again!

He liked the set up. He had Carly on tap at home and every now and again, when the urge hit him, he would have himself a dalliance with someone else. In a bizarre way he thought it kept his and Carly's relationship going. It did until he picked the wrong girl, but that was a situation he couldn't even think about, not then anyway.

Putting his mobile into his pocket; he made his way downstairs following the scent of delicious roast beef. As was tradition in their house from the beginning of time; it was always a family affair. When he had been growing up there had always been quite a gathering around their little dining room table. Mack and his mam; Nan and Granddad, his Uncle Peter and Auntie Lynne, his cousins Ryan and Lou. It had always been Mack's favourite day of the week; the joy of having his cousins there to play with had been great, at the beginning of the day anyway; usually by teatime he was glad to see the back of them; he had spent many a Sunday night sobbing his heart out because one of his toys had been broken. That had been a long time ago; now it was only Christmas that brought his Aunt, Uncle and Cousins to the house. He knew for certain that when he had lived with Carly and they had made plans of their own on a Sunday; there would just be his mam and Granddad sitting at the table! He wished he had visited more!!!

But for that Sunday there would be four of them. Tom and his Granddad were already sitting at the table when he arrived in the dining room. Being there with his little family made him feel better. It didn't really matter that he didn't get the job at Len Pearson Cars; he had a job, and it paid a decent enough wage; it would be more than enough if he could manage his money better. And if he could do that, then he maybe could get himself a better motor on finance! If he was staying at his mam's for the foreseeable future; he may as well make the most of it and do something constructive!

And he found that he actually liked Tom! Not that he hadn't liked him; he just hadn't really spoken to him. They often passed each other at the bathroom door or in the kitchen; but the conversation never really got beyond 'you all right?' 'Aye! You?' He seemed a decent bloke; he had a good job doing something with internet cabling and from what Mack could see; had all his own teeth! When the conversation got around to Tom telling them about what his daughters had been getting up to; he could feel his mam's eyes boring into him! She didn't have to say a word; he could hear her in his head saying; 'just you dare!' That Tom had two daughters virtually the same age as him was news; interesting!

That was something he would bank for a later day when he fancied winding his mam up!

Just as they were finishing up; his mobile rang. Unknown number! He never liked Unknown numbers; not since the Carly thing! Deciding he was just going to ignore it he went to mute the sound; but instead found himself answering it! Len Pearson; no he hadn't got his earlier voicemail! Yes of course he would go to the garage! When? Yep, he would be there in the hour!

(10) CARS   #garynuman

With three pairs of eyes on him; he said that he was off to meet a mate; he didn't think they believed him, they more than likely thought it was some female, but he would let them just think that. He didn't tell them where he was really going because he didn't know why he had been asked to go! Len Pearson had seemed friendly enough; but thinking back over the conversation as he bounded up the stairs to change into something more fitting than football shorts and a scratty tee-shirt, he tried to recall what Len had actually said!

He had told Mack he wanted little chat with him! What sort of little chat though? Could he have found out about Elle and what happened on his desk in his office! Had there been cameras in the room; it was a place of business after all and surely there was money and stuff flying about! Shit; he hadn't even thought to look for CCTV when he had been banging Elle's brains out, not when he thought it had been her office!

Mack did think about not going!! If he was going to be humiliated, then what was the point! But he couldn't be sure that was the reason why Len Pearson had called him; if it was, he would just have to man up and say he didn't know who she was; which was the truth; and he would do what any man would do in that situation; he would strut like a proud peacock! He knew he had been no slouch and if there were cameras, they never lie!

Yet still as he pulled up outside the garage; he felt apprehensive. It was late in the day and again it looked like the garage was closing. As he made his way up to the office, he spotted Len meandering around the cars. Making his way over to him; Len beamed a huge smile at him; certainly not the look of an irate father; he had seen plenty of those looks in his day! He looked pleased to see him!

Whatever it was he had been expecting; it hadn't been to spend the next hour or so wandering around the pitch with Len. He must have been 60 if he was a day; but he seemed to take delight in checking out each of the cars; he blew up tyres; shammied the paint work for scuff marks, but mainly made notes in his little book!

He explained to Mack that he had been selling cars from that spot for over thirty years and that for as long as he could remember he had always come to the pitch on a Sunday afternoon and walked around it! He went on to say that even though all of the stock was all computerised now; and that he had employed a pitch supervisor for years; it didn't do any harm to get out and get dirty himself. It gave him a feel as to how the garage was performing and what was in fashion and what wasn't. Mack was fascinated; he didn't need to do any of this, but there he was wearing an old pair of pants and a garage jacket; blowing up tyres!

When Len was happy that everything that needed to be done had been; they made their way back into the building and sat in the waiting area sipping hot cups of tea poured out of a flask that he had obviously brought from home. 'Another tradition' Len said laughing, 'the wife won't let me leave on a Sunday without it!'

(11) FOUND WHAT I'VE BEEN LOOKING FOR #tomgrennan

Mack was relaxed! He knew for sure that whatever it was Len had wanted to talk to him about it certainly wasn't Elle! But then flabbergasted him by saying that he had been talking about him to the one person he didn't want to be spoken about to. As Len called her, his Eleanor!

Apparently, she had been impressed with him; Mack could feel the feathers of his inner peacock begin to shake! She had thought he was intelligent and pleasant and had been in full agreement about how Mack had described himself as a blank canvas and that they would be able to mould him into the type of salesman they needed; rather than have someone with experience come in and try to sell their own way! Of course Eleanor had gone on to say that he was extremely easy on the eye so that had been a bonus!

Len Pearson was offering him the job. Six month probation period, company car, not a fantastic basic but here were lots of bonuses to be had. Of course he would take the job; he would have to work a month's notice but he had a week's holiday owing so theoretically could start in three weeks! A contract would be in the post for him; a little old fashioned when most things were emailed these days, but he would have been happy if Len Pearson had sent it by carrier pigeon! He had what he had found what he had been looking for and he could not have been happier.

Walking back to his car he was literally strutting like a peacock!

And feeling the need to celebrate he quickly text Melissa; all thoughts of him knocking her on the head as a girlfriend and into the friend zone completely out of the window! Yes she text back she would love a drive out to the coast even if it was a school night! Deal done, he wasn't even bothered about his car when he pulled up outside her house and a beaming Melissa jumped in; three weeks from then he would be driving around in some kind of performance car! He couldn't wait!

Much, much later as he settled himself down in his bed for the night, he felt mint. The trip to the seaside had been good; and for the sake of his old jalopy he'd had one for the road with Melissa! She was small and supple and she could bend into lots of positions he hadn't thought possible in such a small car!

But then somewhere in the moments in between being awake and sleeping; an image of a different bigger car flooded his brain; this time it wasn't the supple Melissa, but Elle Pearson; her long legs straddled across him in the back seat…. there may be trouble ahead he thought as instead of falling asleep the part of him that led him into trouble woke up and sprang into life! He needed to get a grip! But instead took a grip of himself; otherwise, there would be no sleep to be had!!!

(12) LAST FRIDAY NIGHT   #katyperry

Mack's last Friday Night Ritual in the pub was a very rowdy affair. He hadn't wanted one of those traditional leaving dos'; he had been to plenty of those and knew how everyone complained because they felt obliged to go! He didn't want to feel like an obligation; he just wanted to go. But no one ever got away without some kind of a shindig and a gathering in the pub after his last shift seemed as good an idea as any.

It turned out he had to work four weeks' notice; who knew that when your holiday entitlement was four weeks a year; you didn't actually get four weeks unless you had accrued them! With two weeks in Ibiza and a week off when he moved back into his mam's under his belt; he had no option but either work the extra week or lose a week's pay! Len Pearson said he was happy to wait the extra week and change the offer of contract accordingly.

It had been a funny old four weeks. Everyone was shocked and pleased for him in what seemed to be equal measures! His mam was as proud as punch; his friends all wanted mates' rates and the people he worked with were all in agreement that he would certainly do well selling cars and all the benefits that went with it. He pretended he didn't know what they meant; but the memory of Elle Pearson and the interview that wasn't an interview was still as clear as if it had just happened yesterday!

Full of nervous energy; he stepped up his visits to the gym. Convincing himself that it was just to burn up some of the energy; he knew in reality it was to make sure that he turned up for his first day at Len Pearson Cars in his very best physical shape! If Elle Pearson thought he was easy on the eye, he had better make sure that he was.

He was vain; he was a product of a generation where a bloke took their grooming as seriously as any woman would. He had his hair cut every three weeks to the day and the stubble that looked like a 5 o'clock shadow; was meticulously trimmed every morning. His body was lean and toned due to the gym and Sunday League football and the training sessions that ensured during the footie season and whereas some of the lads at the gym liked to keep their chests waxed; Mack liked to have the au natural look; women loved it.

If he said so himself; he had always been a looker. There were old photographs of him as a baby and toddler, he was cute then. But even in his teens he never went through the teeth too big for your mouth; sticky out ears or spots phase. He was a natural, even if he had been a little on the short side when he went into his teens; by the time he was 15, he was touching 6ft. It was around that time he started to notice the opposite sex; he had always had a lot of friends who were girls, but as his height grew; so, did his popularity. And girls were always keen to show him just how much they liked him.

(13) UNDERNEATH YOUR CLOTHES   #shakira

Mack was always a gentleman though; even at that young age. He never bragged to his mates about any of the girls that he had learned the joy of sex and everything that went with it; he had heard other lads doing it and always thought it sounded pathetic; especially when they would compare the girls and decided which was good with her mouth or who had nice tits. Maybe it was because of his mam and how she had brought him up; he just wasn't the type to kiss and tell.

He was no saint though; he was a horny little shit and if it was on offer; he was having it no matter who they were. His appetite for women had no boundaries; it was a big adventure to him; an adventure that he was still on; he might have calmed down for a little while but the urge to travel to new places was always there; if he was a girl he would have been labelled a slag; the worst he had been called was a player and a cheat. His mates thought he was a hero; especially the ones who were married with children; they treated him like he was some kind of sex God!

He had Googled what a sex addict was; he didn't think the definition related too much to him. He didn't watch porn unless he was in company and they were using it for titillation; he certainly didn't get moody if he didn't get sex and he didn't masturbate more than was deemed normal or have any weird fetish! As far as he could see; he liked women and the buzz he got from them, but he mainly liked the chase and the beginning of a relationship. He liked nothing better than getting with a female for the first time and seeing what was underneath their clothes!

The only problem he had, if he did have a problem, was once he had actually seen what was underneath their clothes, it was time for a new challenge. Carly had been an exception. They had been friends for so long before they got together, he didn't want to risk their friendship by sleeping with her then moving on. He had actually loved her; he still did, or as much as he could love someone whose life he had virtually destroyed. Every argument she had put to him about why they shouldn't have been together had come true. She had been right! His mam had been right! He might have loved the idea of settling down and sharing his life with one woman; but in truth he had been nowhere near ready! The proof had been in the pudding!

Maybe that was why Elle Pearson was still in his thoughts; she hadn't taken her clothes off; she had just hitched her dress up and pulled down her knickers! It was still there for him; the tingle. She may be unfinished business and the thought of seeing her again at work was as exciting as starting the job itself!

And Melissa was still around; still just friend material; but as it stood she was very much a friend with benefits. Whether it was because he knew he was moving on at work, or maybe he genuinely enjoyed her company, either way he had spent a fair old amount of time with her, so much time that people at work were talking. Could she be the one? No way Mack still can't be still talking to one of his conquests?? The chitter chatter went on and on! His only hope was that Melissa didn't read too much into it and think that they were actually going somewhere!!

Mack was well aware he was a shit; he had been called it often enough off very many people. But to be fair to him; he had never said anything to Melissa about them being an item. His reputation preceded him and he was under no illusion that the many females he had dallied with in the Call Centre would have put young Melissa straight on Mack and his inability to stay faithful.

He was having a good time with her. She was up for anything; they had been on numerous shopping trips to get Mack kitted out for his new job! It turned out to be a costly task; he had a couple of suits but they were ones that he had bought for weddings; christenings and funerals and weren't very workwearish!

So over the space of three weekends; he bought a new suit along with what seemed like two dozen shirts and ties and some smarts trousers and shoes. He was sure that L Pearson would supply him with coats and fleeces so held back from buying jackets until he got there! It had cost a small fortune, but he liked the thought of getting dressed in a shirt and tie in a morning instead of wearing jeans and sweatshirts like he did now! First impressions were everything and he wanted to leave a lasting impression on everyone; staff and customers. Start as he meant to go on!

(14) 99 RED BALLOONS   #nena

His contract had arrived in the post. It was all written clearly and concisely. He read through it once signed it; put it in the self-addressed envelope provided and sent it straight back. If there had been any small print; it had been so small he had missed it! But he would have signed it anyway! He couldn't wait!

Len Pearson had called him a couple of times; his hunch had been right and he was being provided with a jacket, so Len had wanted to know what size! That had been the first phone call; the second was really exciting! Mack's car would be ready for him to pick up the day before he was due to start work; if he called just before closing time on the Sunday; he would be able to take his company car then and wouldn't have to worry about getting a lift to work on the Monday or being stuck with two cars. They just needed to have a copy of his driving licence and he would be good to go!

Mack's excitements knew no bounds!

And he had been really touched on his last shift at work. There had been balloons and a card signed off so many people; it must have gone around the whole building. And there had obviously been a whip round; Burton's vouchers; and a lot of them; who ever had organised the present had put some thought into it and got him something useful. More new work clothes he thought to himself as he as he thanked everyone who had made their way to the staff room to wish him well!

Later at the pub, he lost count of the amount of hands he shook and cheeks he kissed; he was genuinely moved by all of the good wishes. He hadn't realised how well liked he was, but he had no regrets about leaving them; there was greener grass to be had!

As per usual; he stayed at Melissa's! Whether it was because it was probably his last Friday night with her; he really couldn't see them meeting up when he wasn't seeing her at work 5 days a week; but then again, he had seen her on his days off so he couldn't really say for sure. Anyway, he decided if it was their last night together he was going to make it as special as possible. She had been so sweet to him the past few weeks; he was probably making a rod for his own back; but he would deal with it as and when; for that night it wasn't just about the sex; it was about making it a night she wouldn't forget! He hoped he had achieved it; she was either an aspiring porn star or he really had hit the spot!

Melissa did her customary lift back home to his mam's house the next morning; he actually felt a little wave of sadness pass over him; he probably wouldn't see her again; or at least not see her for a long time. She didn't know any of this; she would probably assume that they would hook up the next week; but Mack had no intention; not at that point anyway. He never said never!

(15) ALL GOES WRONG   #chaseandstatus

His mam was as great believer if something was meant to be then it would happen, no matter how hopeless it seemed at the time. She always said that we had to be patient and what was right for us would manifest itself; people; money; career. What we were meant to be or need would somehow travel the universe and end up in our lives! If they didn't, then they weren't meant to be there in the first place!

So if you said goodbye to someone and your really didn't want them to go; then if it had been a mistake; they would come back to you and all would be well. If they didn't, then it was goodbye to bad rubbish. That was his mam; Paula's philosophy for life. Mack couldn't have lived with her for the majority of his life without some of her rubbing off on him! So as he kissed Melissa goodbye that Saturday morning; he said a little sorry to the God's of Fate for casting her aside and with the promise that if she found her way back to him; he would pay attention. She really was nice!

His mam had lived her life according to the laws of Fate. When his dad had run out on them when Mack was still only a few months old; Paula had decided that if her absent boyfriend was worth having he would be back. She had concentrated on making a life for her and her baby and though she said she had missed Phillip, she wasn't going to let it ruin her life. He had panicked when Mack was born; they were young and the responsibility of having a tiny life to take care of was all a bit too much for him and he had gone!

Paula on the other hand loved Mack with all of her heart, he was the centre of her world. With the help of his Nan and Granddad; Paula had got a full-time job and worked her backside off to make sure Mack had everything he needed. Phillip did come back; there were photographs in the box in his mam's room to prove it. Birthdays; Christmas, a picture of them all on the beach. But by the time Mack started school he was gone altogether and any memories he might have had of his dad were only prompted by the photographs.

He had found out where his dad was a few years ago quite by accident. But that was a story for another day; it could have turned out very differently and not in a good way! Even though he knew where he was; Mack had never been tempted to go and actually meet him. He didn't resent his dad or anything; there just never seemed to be a good enough reason. He knew for sure that his mam had always kept in touch; he knew that the school photographs that were ordered were always done in duplicate and one of them would be posted off. Mack had never asked; but who else would it be!

Phillip had gone on and had another family; this Mack knew for a fact due to the accidental not to be spoken about event; at least one-half sister; there may have been others. Maybe one day he would go and say hello; but his mam had always been enough. She had been the one who had run up and down the touch line when he played football; she was the one who had gone without herself so he could go on one of those costly school trips and it would always be her and her feelings that would determine whether Mack ever had a relationship with Phillip!

The truth of it was he had been having a kind of relationship with him. We he was younger he had asked his mam over and over what his dad looked like. She used to always think long and hard about it; but she would always come back to the same person; 'Mack your dad is the double of the lead singer of The Housemartins!' Always impressed his dad had maybe not movies star looks, but certainly them of a musician; he would stare for hours at the little pictures on the CD's of The Housemartins and then later The Beautiful South his mam had in her huge music collection. That could be my dad; Mack used to think as he stared and stared at the dismantled CD covers!

The strange thing was he loved The Housemartins; whether by taste or the fact he felt some sort of affinity with them. It didn't matter, Paul Heaton's music travelled everywhere with him! Happy Hour was Mack's karaoke song; low and behold if anyone chose it before he got chance to sing it; he couldn't sing for toffee; but with all of the years of practice; he did a pretty mean rendition of Paul Heaton's vocal on the track. He loved the fact that it was something he shared with his dad; whether it be fact or fiction; and when he sang it; he always managed to have the room jumping. But looks wise; his dad looked like Paul Heaton?? Really??

(16) HAPPY HOUR   #thehousemartins

And then it was Sunday. The day before he started his new job! More importantly it was new car day! He was up early and outside cleaning and polishing his little old car. He hadn't known what to do with it, so had asked his Granddad if he could put it back in his garage for the time being; if it didn't work out at Len Pearson Cars, he would be needing it again. So for the time being, it was going back into its little box for another day. Obviously, his Granddad would have a dickie fit if he saw how scruffy it was; the bodywork was still in pretty good shape; but the inside was a tip and it took Mack a couple of hours decluttering before he dared leave it in his Granddad's tender care.

Another Sunday roast with pleasant conversation over the dinner table, then him and his Granddad were off to drop the little car off and then the plan was for his Granddad to drop Mack off at the garage to pick up his new motor!

Then they were there; his new workplace. The bunting was fluttering in the wind and as he made his way up the pitch, he spotted Len Pearson carrying out his usual Sunday afternoon ritual of checking his pitch. He looked delighted to see Mack and for the next half hour or so they ambled around the pitch together as Len checked everything was just as it should be with each car; and explained what the next few weeks would have in store for his young protégé! All the while Mack was conscious of his Granddad sitting outside the garage in his car; he had insisted. Said he wanted to make sure the Mack got home safely in his strange car; said he may as well as he was going back to his mam's for his tea anyway! But it had been a while now; Mack hoped his Granddad had sense to sit with the engine running to keep his car warm!

Eventually they made their way into the office block and Len darted into the office to collect Mack's car keys. All was sorted he said; Mack was on the company insurance and although he didn't have him a fuel card yet; the vehicle was almost full and there should be enough in for the next few days. Len went on to explain that while the vehicle was at the premises; it would always have a Sale Board on; so could he make sure that was always on show when he left the vehicle in a morning; and that it was always in a saleable state; tidy inside and out. Apart from that; he was free to use it at his will and could keep it until it sold or the mileage got a bit too high!

Mack's excitement bubbled. Len Pearson went on; 'I heard you had your eye on it, so thought, why not? We hope your going to be with us for a long time!' they made their way back down the pitch to the main gates; there was a line of cars parked and Mack pressed the button on the keys remote. A shiny four-wheel drive crew cab sprang into life; it was the one with the shiny chrome he had clocked the night of his interview! He couldn't believe it.

Elle Pearson must have been watching him on the cameras; he had halted only for a second debating whether to go over to it to have a closer look! But she must have seen him!

As he jumped in the truck, thanking Len and telling him he was looking forward to the next day, he couldn't stop grinning. He hadn't drove anything else apart from his car and his driving instructors; he hadn't even drove any of his mam's cars! This was huge and had so many gadgets he didn't really know where to start. He jumped back out of the car and ran across to where his Granddad was waiting patiently; he really didn't want him following him back to his mam's, so telling him that he had to go back into the garage and sign some paperwork; he sent him on his way; with the promise of a ride around the block when he got home!

Back in the car, he started the engine and while the truck purred away; he familiarised himself where everything he needed was. Bluetooth; the car even had Bluetooth. Pairing his mobile; he found the track he was looking for; he released the handbrake and slowly made his way off the kerb and along the street.

He hit the play button and the cab was filled with the sound of his 'would be father' *'and it's happy hour again, I think I might be happy.........*

(17) 9 – 5   #dollyparton

Mack's first few hours at Len Pearson Cars was unexpectedly boring!

He hadn't been sure what to expect but he hadn't thought he would be sitting at an unfamiliar desk, nursing a tepid cup of coffee for what seemed liked an eternity. It had been a bumper weekend at the garage and everyone seemed to be flat out doing whatever it was they did.

He hadn't seen anything of Len Pearson. Apparently, Mondays was one of his buying days and he didn't usually arrive at the garage until lunchtime. Mack had known this; he had told Mack that he would be meeting John when he arrived, and he would show him around and introduce him to everyone. So far, all John had done was plonk him at a desk which he presumed would be his; then give him some sheets of paper to have a read through.

Having never been to the garage during regular working hours; Mack was surprised at the amount of people who worked there. There was lots of hustle and bustle; shouting and the telephone never seemed to stop ringing. He felt like a book end; he thought about helping with the phones; but they only seemed to ring a couple of times and then they were answered; there was obviously a receptionist somewhere picking the calls up; but he hadn't seen anyone.

The sheets of paper were all information about the garage. There were holiday forms; sick procedure; a couple of forms to complete regarding next of kin and another requesting his bank details for his wages. There was an Organisation Chart which looked more like a family tree; but it advertised itself as a family business so what else could he expect. He took a good look at it: -

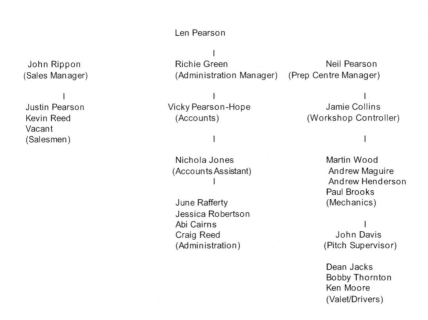

Len Pearson
|

John Rippon (Sales Manager)	Richie Green (Administration Manager)	Neil Pearson (Prep Centre Manager)
Justin Pearson Kevin Reed Vacant (Salesmen)	Vicky Pearson-Hope (Accounts)	Jamie Collins (Workshop Controller)
	Nichola Jones (Accounts Assistant)	Martin Wood Andrew Maguire Andrew Henderson Paul Brooks (Mechanics)
	June Rafferty Jessica Robertson Abi Cairns Craig Reed (Administration)	John Davis (Pitch Supervisor)
		Dean Jacks Bobby Thornton Ken Moore (Valet/Drivers)

Mack scoured the chart over and over; there certainly was a lot of Pearson's' on it; but there was one very big exception; Eleanor Pearson!

Was she not Len's right hand man? He had been nervous all morning about seeing her; nervous nervous and nice nervous! He had been up really early; took his time getting ready so he knew he would be looking his best when he saw her at work! But not only had he not seen her; it didn't even look as if she worked there. He couldn't work out if he was disappointed or relieved!

It was a new sensation for Mack; there weren't many women who got under his skin; especially ones who he had spent so little time with. But Elle Pearson had been something else; if he had told his mates about her, they would say she had chocolate flavoured tits. Obviously this was a term of endearment; what they really meant was she was a good shag!

Maybe she was; but it was more the fact that she had taken control of a situation and that didn't happen very often for Mack. Even when girls made it very clear that they wanted to have sex with him; he was always in control. Very rarely did Mack do anything he didn't want to; girls might have thought that it was them running the show; but he was good at reading people and sometimes it paid to let them think that they were in the driving seat!

He could count the amount of times on one hand that he had not been in control with a female. They were some of the best times; but it seldom happened like that. He was big and strong and women always seemed to dance to his tune rather than the other way around. The first time he met someone who was his match and more was when he was still a teenager! He was no blushing virgin; he had been with lots and lots of girls by then and probably had all the strut of a young buck who thought they knew it all. She was older; much older and he had always had a bit of a bee in his bonnet about her!

(18) STACEY'S MOM   #fountainsofwayne

To his shame; he had slept with the daughter first; and for the purpose of not naming and shaming anyone; let's just call her Stacey. It had been years earlier; and it had been one of those things that you have at a party when your young; but because they had been all the way through school together; he knew who her mam was, she was a head turner.

His mates used to actually drool when they saw her on parents evening; and Mack had to agree; she was one hot momma! Whereas most mams turned up looking like mams; she turned up looking like a super model! She would clip clop into the school hall in her stilettos; leaving a waft of Chanel No.5 as she passed by.

Even if she was with her equally beautiful husband; the male teachers would all watch her with their tongues hanging out; and if they were lucky enough to be one of her daughter's teachers, well that made the usual tedium of the parents evening all worthwhile; Stacy's Mom really had it going on!

Poor Stacy; she really did get some stick about her mam; the kids; the teachers! It seemed everyone wanted a piece of her mam and to her credit, she took it all in good fun. But when some of girls started to ask her if she was adopted and that her mam and dad couldn't be her parents; Mack knew things had gone too far and that was probably the reason he had singled her out at the party and slept with her.

But Stacy's Mom had been something else. He could remember everything about her as clear as day; even though it had been years since he had seen her. He had been out with some workmates in the City Centre when one of them leaned over and told him there was some hot bird watching him.

Mack wasn't fazed; the mates he was out with were newish ones he had met at the Call Centre and it was the first time they had all been out together. Not wanting to blow his own trumpet or appear arrogant; it happened all of the time. He looked older than his young years; even back then he had his 5 o'clock shadow; no one was sporting beards back then.

He did the customary turn around to see who the fuss was all about and was taken aback when he saw who it was. Stacy's Mom! She looked as hot as ever; if it was possible even hotter! She beamed a smile at him and beckoned him over!

After a few pleasantries about how he was and what he was doing; she leant over and whispered into his ear! The music was loud and he wasn't sure if he had heard her right!

Not sure what he should do; he smiled and nodded; which seemed to be the correct answer because she grabbed him by the hand and made her way through the crowd and out of the pub!

With a glance back at his mates he was going to shout he wouldn't be long; but the look on their faces was priceless so he just grinned and left!

(19) SECRET LOVER   #tomgrennan

Not really knowing what was going on; he was shocked when she made her way up the road and through the gates of what looked like a small park. He hadn't noticed it ever being there; but he wasn't a city boy and apart from shopping trips; nights in the pubs or football matches at St James Park; he didn't really know the city centre.

It was late; very late and there was no one around. As they kept walking; Mack could make out the shadowy shapes of the swings and slides; she didn't say a word, just kept tight a hold of his hand as she strided out in her stilettoes; unexpectedly agile in such an inappropriate footwear for the uneven terrain.

When they got to the darkest corner she stopped and turned to face him! Before he knew what was going on she was on her knees and pulling down the zip on his jeans. The air felt cold as she took out what she wanted; she didn't need to wake it up; he was ready for her. He had been since he saw her in the pub. And then it was hot! Her mouth was so hot!

It didn't end there though. The cold air hit him again; he was pleased; he was losing control. She was wearing jeans; tight ones, but they were down and she was leaning towards the wall; using her hands to keep her upright! And then it was hot again; so very very hot!

When it was over she asked him if he had his mobile with him. He pulled it out of his pocket and handed it to her. He still hadn't said a word! She used it for a few minutes; tapping away; she gave it him back and then kissing him gently on the mouth she started heading back in the direction they had come.

If she was frightened about being in a deserted park in the middle of the night she didn't show it. Mack followed along behind; by the time he got out of the park and made his way back towards the pub he could see her in the distance flagging down a taxi and jumping in.

As it drove past him he looked in it to wave to her, but she wasn't looking; her head was pointed dead straight ahead. If she had seen Mack she certainly didn't acknowledge him!

It was the biggest sexual buzz he had ever had; up until then anyway!

He checked his phone; there was nothing. He had thought that she was giving him her mobile number; but there were no new numbers! He couldn't think what she had been doing. Stacy's Mom; who would ever have thought it!

It didn't end there though. A few weeks later an unknown number messaged him. It wasn't so much a request more of an order. Time; place along with post code, of course he was going!

It was a remote picnic area, as he pulled his little car into the car park she got out of her car. It was every lad's fantasy; very high heels again; long coat, but underneath the coat there was very little.

It was so sexy!

He wasn't there long; just long enough for Mack to confirm that Stacy's Mom was the hottest woman on the planet!

His dalliance with Stacy's Mom went on like that for a couple of months. There was never any chit chat. Message; meeting and very sexy sex!

She always smelled of Chanel No.5; sometimes if he got a waft of it nowadays, images of her would flood his mind; not that he ever forgot her; she was very much part of his 'wank bank,'

He was never sure what she was all about!

She obviously liked the control she had over him; while he was having his thing with her, every other girl seemed to pale into insignificance; not that he kept himself for her; he never knew when she was going to want him; and a boy had needs. But for that short amount of time he was totally enthralled by her; even a little bit obsessed and totally her puppy!

Then the messages just stopped. Mack was tempted to text her and ask her what was going on; but he had pride and if she didn't want him anymore that was fine. He deleted her number, he didn't want to give himself opportunity to drop her a text when he had had too much to drink one night. If that was that then that was that.

But she had given him a penchant for a dominating woman. Not dominatrix; he didn't want to be hurt, just women who were in control of themselves and of him; it was his thing!

And high heels were most definitely his thing. Elle Pearson had worn them and look what had happened there!!

He never saw Stacy's Mom again!'

(20) TWO PINTS OF LAGER   #splodgenessabounds

It was almost lunchtime before John eventually managed to make some time for him. He apologised over and over for not getting to Mack sooner; but it had been a mad weekend and he had lots to sort out to make sure the sold cars were ready for their new owners.

First things first John said; a tour of the garage and introductions to everyone. It was much bigger than it had looked from the outside, there were garages and garages to the rear of the premises; more offices and valet bays. The cars that were sold were all kept there until it was time for them to be collected or delivered; and the new stock was all parked up there waiting to go through the process of getting them ready to be put up for sale on the pitch.

And all the while Mack was being introduced to this one and that one. He tried to make a mental note who was who and what their role was; but it would take time.

He hated being the new boy!

By the time he got back to his desk he was a little punch drunk; more paperwork had been left for him while he had been away and John explained that there was always a new stock list issued on a Monday; but it was ever evolving so it would be easier if he showed him the system they used and started explaining how everything worked.

At some time during the afternoon Len popped his head in and said hello; but for the remainder of the day; he made notes and tried to suss out how the whole thing worked. When John suggested a pint on their way home Mack jumped at the chance.

John was a gossip; he may have been his boss, but Mack very quickly realised that this bloke wasn't to be trusted. He had loose lips; and like his mam always said to him; loose lips sink ships! It would be very unlikely that Mack would strike up a friendship with John Rippon.

It turned out that John Rippon had been head hunted by Len. When his last Sales Manager had retired; John Rippon had been suggested by a mutual acquaintance as a successor and Len Pearson had made him an offer he couldn't refuse. But even sitting with him in the pub for an hour, Mack thought him a little too full of himself. He was under no illusion that John would be very good at his job; he had patter and obviously knew the car trade extensively; but in the short time they spent together in the pub; Mack knew that you couldn't tell him anything you wouldn't want talked about!

In John's words Len Pearson was a good bloke. But also in John's words; he should be retired by now. Apparently it was a young man's game these days; it was a lot more regulated than it had ever been; and well Len Pearson was old school. If there was a deal to be done; then it should be done by any means; that wasn't always feasible in today's climate; where the customer had rights and if there was an issue with the car after their customer had taken delivery and then chose to reject it; no stone would be unturned in the pursuit of making the garage buy the car back. Len's ways could not sustain such rigorous examination!

The garage, according to John Rippon, would be better in a younger man's hands; someone who had the qualifications to make sure even the shadiest of deals stayed within the expected remit. Someone like John Rippon, Mack thought to himself as he listened to his new boss go on about Len Pearson on a more personal level.

Hurtling towards his 70's; Len Pearson's current wife was wife number 4. It was a shock to Mack; thinking back to the tea and flask when he had gone in to see Len Pearson the day he had offered him the job; Mack had very much been given the impression that Len and his Mrs had been together forever. But no; John said they had been married maybe five years at most, but there had most definitely been 3 wives before her and numerous girlfriends.

Len Pearson was a dark horse. Len Pearson Cars hadn't always been Len Pearson Cars; it had once been J P Knight Used Car Dealership. Len Pearson's first wife was Joan Knight; only child of James Knight; the original proprietor. By all intense and purposes; when Len married Joan; he also became James Knight's right-hand man and a few years later when James Knight died of a heart attack; the business went to his daughter and her husband. Len Pearson revamped the garage and the rest as they say is history.

(21) DARK HORSE   #katyperry

The marriage didn't last though; Joan Knight had always been spoilt off her more than generous father; Len wasn't made from the same cloth and believed in investing his money wisely rather than flying off around the world on expensive holidays or constantly renewing her wardrobe.

The cracks in the marriage quickly appeared and just as quickly Joan Knight decided she wanted to go and live in America; something Len Pearson would not even think about. The garage had been doing surprisingly well with Len at the helm; so he went to the bank; got a considerable loan and paid Joan off. He then waved her off and had never seen her again. Before the divorce even came through; Len was living with Lucy, a barmaid who worked at his local pub around the corner from his garage.

Neil was born shortly after; but it was another doomed relationship. Lucy had only ever worked in a pub; pretty as a picture and did amazing things to Len; or at least he thought they were amazing after only having experienced a rather sour faced Joan, but in fact it seemed she had done amazing things to lots of other people and seemed to think as Len wasn't her husband then she could still do them.

Len had set her up in a nice little house and saw Neil as often as he could. Then along came Jackie! The second Mrs Pearson; stepmother to Neil and mother to Jayne.

She had been on another level from the first two women in Len's life; smart and very smart; Len thought he had hit the jackpot with this one and he had to a certain extent. They had a good life together; business was going well; Len had managed to secure a piece of land at the rear of the garage and spent the previous year extending the workshops so instead of out sourcing mechanical work to nearby garages; they could employ their own staff and have a more comprehensive; cost effective service.

But maybe he expected too much. Maybe he thought she would be happy staying at home and bringing up Jayne and more often than not Neil who was dumped on her wily nilly whenever Lucy couldn't be bothered with him or had something else to do. Whatever the reason Jackie changed. Their once rampant relationship dwindled to a customary shag once a week; with little enthusiasm from Jackie; it felt like she was only doing it out of a sense of duty!

(22) HERE I GO AGAIN   #whitesnake

Mack couldn't believe how much information John Rippon knew about Len Pearson and his life. But it was a small business and people tended to confide in the people they spent the most time with and although Mack thought that probably the bones of what he had been told were true; John was laying the flesh on them!

They never got to what happened to Jackie Pearson and her diminishing affection for her husband. John's phone rang and it was obviously Mrs Rippon asking his whereabouts and estimated time of arrival home; because no sooner had he ended the call then they were on their feet and making their way out of the pub. No doubt there would be many more nights where John would fill in the missing pieces of the Len Pearson Story!

Back in his truck Mack felt twitchy. He wasn't ready for going home; he could feel the familiar tug in his pants! He hated to do it and knew he shouldn't but what else could he do! A man had needs!

An hour later parked up in the picnic area he had long ago met up with Stacy's Mom; Mack impressed Melissa with the versatility of having a huge truck! By all accounts he impressed her at least three times; she really was a nice girl.

Again he threw her back to the Gods of Fate as he dropped her off outside her house!

He was a shit; he knew that and he shouldn't have called her, but she was no bother and his head had been full of a combination of Stacy' Mom and Elle Pearson; a combination that gave him a hard on he knew he wouldn't have been able to fully satisfy on his own. But he had to stop this thing with Melissa; he was fond of her, but he knew she was becoming more than fond of him.

On an impulse he pulled out his phone and deleted her number.

As he edged away from the house; he gave a little glance at the front door; there she was standing waving him off! There was no doubt about it; he was a complete and utter twat.

(23) BRIGHT FUTURE IN SALES   #sugahboat

By the Friday of the first week Mack was feeling a bit more at home working at Len Pearson Cars. He hadn't sold a car; and he still didn't really know what he was doing. But he had shadowed the other salesmen and felt sure that if he had to; he could fumble his way through a sale. But of course fumbling wasn't Mack's style.

If he was going to do car sales for a living then he wanted to be good at it. So he asked Justin and Kevin; the other salesmen lots and lots of questions; he made notes and he watched everything that went on around him.

He studied John! He may not have been Mack's cup of tea mate wise; but he certainly knew his onions. His literally knew the price of every car on the pitch and in most cases the cars complete spec. He knew if customers who came onto the pitch had bought cars before; recently or sometime in the past and more often than not; if they had bought before, he knew what car they had bought. Mack was a little bit in awe of him. Somehow everything in the garage went through John and thinking back to the conversation they had had earlier in the week at the pub; Mack was in no doubt that John Rippon rightly thought when Len Pearson retired; he would be the right man for the job.

The other two salesmen; were good, not in the same league as John but very much part of the team. Mack liked them both instantly; he had only met Kevin briefly on Monday and didn't see Justin at all until the Wednesday; but they seemed to be happy he was there; by all accounts Mack's predecessor had been a knob and had left under a cloud, but he didn't pry. Somehow he got the feeling that garage gossip would fill him in sometime in the not too distant future.

Kevin Reed looked to be in his early forties; he must have been his son also worked in the business but much to Kevin's dismay he was a receptionist and totally as camp as Christmas. As soon as Kevin had told Mack his son worked in admin he immediately knew who he was talking about. He had met him on his initial walkaround meeting everyone; Craig might have been on a call when John told him who he was and what he did; but it certainly didn't stop Craig giving Mack a lingering look and actually licking his lips!! Oh yes; Craig Reed was one for Mack to keep an eye on!

Happy with his sexuality he didn't mind being pursued by someone of the same sex! As sexual as Mack was; men just didn't do it for him. But he appreciated anyone who appreciated him and was always careful not to cause offence; and Kevin Reed was hysterical when talking about his son. He took the micky out of him something rotten; but underneath all of the bravado; Mack sensed that Kevin loved his son very much and was proud of him for being the person he was!

Kevin himself had worked at the garage for about seven years. He had arrived there when the specialist garage he had worked at had gone pop and his next door neighbour at the time a bloke called Ken had put a word in with Len Pearson for him. With his expertise in performance cars; Len Pearson had snapped him up and together they had worked to ensure that there was always a selection of the expensive specialist cars that customers would travel far and wide for!

It had turned out to be a very lucrative side to the business. Kevin helped Len source cars which sometimes needed a considerable amount of work carried out to them before they could be put up for sale; but those cars were always purchased at knock down prices and once repaired and restored to their former glory could be sold at extortionate prices! Kevin loved his job; the prestige cars were only a small part of his day to day business; the rest of the time he was part of the team;

though low and behold any team member who thought about selling one of his cars for themselves!

(24) WORK   #rihanna

Justin Pearson was what it said on the tin. He was a Pearson. Nephew of Len Pearson, but if Mack thought because he was a Pearson he was privileged; he couldn't be more wrong. Apparently in the workplace if you had a Pearson surname then you tended to be one of the whipping boys! Justin wasn't much older than Mack and had worked at the garage since leaving school although only on the sales team for the past year or so. Previously he had been part of the valet/driving team; and according to Justin, that's the way it was for the Pearsons. There was no leg up; they started at the bottom and if they did get promoted then it was through hard work and not birth-right!

Mack thought he was all right though; from what he learned about him in the first week. He was happy to sit and show Mack how things worked; he dragged him out to customers on the pitch, introduced him and even let him sign up customers finance documents by the end of the week. He had the patience of Jobe with Mack.

Having only recently moved in with his girlfriend; he was happily invited Mack to his housewarming party the following weekend. Their newly acquired flat was the size of a Corsa according to Justin; so instead of them having the party at their place; they were having it at a pub down the street. So not so much a housewarming more come and celebrate us starting to live together party. Housewarming gifts were optional but would be very appreciated; according to Justin they didn't have a pot to piss in which Mack thought was hysterical seeing as from what he had seen of the Pearsons so far; they all seemed to be loaded.

All in all the week had gone well. He my not have been rocking the world of car sales; but he was learning and he had a grasp of the basics so that was a start. If he could get a couple of sales under his belt he would feel better; but they seemed loathe to let him loose and he had to satisfy himself shadowing the others and doing bits of admin work for them.

Which brought him into contact with the lovely Nichola Jones; Accounts Assistant. She was the go-to person when finance documents had been signed; and seeing as for the majority of the week he had been everyone else's 'go-for' he had quite a lot of dealings with her

(25) CRUSH   #jenniferpaige

And boy was she a flirt!

One look at Mack and he was on her radar. She wasted no time in telling anyone who would listen how tall dark and handsome the new starter in Sales was; a bit of eye candy for the ladies! The banter went on and on with her; and to her credit she was funny with it. She was maybe about thirty; a touch younger perhaps and had worked in the accounts department part-time since she had her little boy three years earlier. Her desk was some kind of shrine to her toddler; there were photographs everywhere; holiday; Christmas; Halloween; the little boy was obviously her world.

She wore a wedding ring but there was no mention of Mr Jones. Mack had worked with plenty of women to know which ones were happy at home and which ones weren't. Nichola Jones showed all of the signs of having an unhappy relationship at home. By the time the week was out Mack was under no disillusion that Mrs Jones was crushing on him.

He had accepted her friend request on Facebook and he had taken her mobile number just as he had everyone else who had offered theirs to him that week, whereas he had the feeling everyone else would only contact him if necessary; and vice versa!

Nichola Jones had texted him the same night she had got his number. It was all welcome; welcome; welcome, but Mack wasn't stupid and there were definitely undercurrents of something else. He didn't mind; he was happy chit chatting with her; her texts were funny and informative about his new work colleagues. He probably found out more about the people at work off her while he sat watching Top Gear at home than he did actually being at work.

And she wasn't bad looking on the eye either. She certainly wasn't mumsy; she dressed trendy and although there weren't any high heels on show; she had pretty long legs which was always a plus in Mack's book!

(26) ONE FOR THE ROAD   #artic monkeys

He hadn't been expecting a Friday Night ritual in the pub; but as they closed up everyone who was left for the close of play agreed they would see each other in 5 minutes down the road. It was date night for his mam and Tom at home so having a couple of pints and whiling away and hour wouldn't go a miss.

Nowhere near the amount of people who used to meet up for the Call Centre Friday Night Ritual; there was still a few around the table when Mack sat down with his pint. They were all male, but there was John, Kevin and Justin from the sales who in their own words said they were always at work from dawn til dusk.   Jamie who looked after the Workshop and a couple of the Valeters; Ken and Dean. The chat was all of football and Newcastle United's upcoming match that weekend; and the state of their position in the league. Beyond that there wasn't really much else. Another pint and then they were all dispersing and heading home. Most of them were at work again the next day.

Happy that Mack was starting to fit in; he thought about ringing one of his mates and seeing if he fancied going for a curry or something. It was still far too early to be going home!! Mobile in hand he had messages. Even though he had never been told to keep his mobile on silent; it was an old habit from his previous job that you kept your phone quiet and out of sight during working hours. He had messages. Nichola Jones!!

Did he want to call at hers for a coffee and catch up??? Did he??? He wasn't sure. He knew she fancied him!! Did that matter!! There was a child and Mr Jones so even if she did fancy him she had commitments in other areas and maybe she was just being friendly. But did he want a coffee and a catch up?? She was good crack; and would he even manage to grab one of his mates for a curry; it was well gone 8 o'clock now!! He didn't want to go home; not yet anyway, just in case his mam and Tom were being really friendly; there seemed to be an unspoken rule since he moved back home; Mack going home on a Friday night before 11 was a no no!

So yes he would have a coffee and a catch up with the very lovely Nichola Jones! Within minutes he had her post code in his built in Sat Nav and the truck was heading off in her direction.

And twenty minutes later he was standing on her doorstep ringing the bell.

Nichola Jones answered the door with her usually tied up hair tumbling over her shoulders. Long and brunette; she looked so much prettier with it when it was down and loose. She wore jeans and a t-shirt and she had only a smidgen of make-up and Mack was surprised to see that she had lots of little freckles all over her nose. Sun kisses, not freckles!!

She was the perfect host. She made coffee and supplied a packet of chocolate biscuits for them to dunk into their cups. Her little boy was staying the night with her mam as it was Nichola's Saturday in to work, which turned out to be on a one in four rotas; something else Mack learnt.

When it was suggested they had a proper drink Mack wasn't sure! He had already had two pints in the pub, another may push him over the edge for driving home. But then she was there with a bottle of wine and two glasses and he didn't have the heart to refuse when she filled the glasses and placed one in front of him. He didn't have to drink it, he could just have a few sips and then leave it!

But the conversation flowed and as the gossip got juicer; Mack found himself drinking the glass without really thinking about it. The refill came and he started on that one too. Nichola was good fun; she knew everything about everyone that worked at Pearson's. Who was nice; who wasn't so nice! It was all trivial stuff; nowhere near the depth of knowledge about people that John Rippon had, but still it was good to know about the people he had started work with.

The bottle of wine was empty! He hadn't finished his second glass, but still he probably had drunk too much to be driving his lovely shiny truck. More coffee was on offer; it had only just turned ten; still a bit too early for home, but by the time he drank his coffee he would be able to make his way slowly home; and the coffee wouldn't do him any harm diluting the lager and wine mix!

(27) BREAKING UP IS HARD TO DO   #neilsedaka

While she made the coffee, he took the opportunity to have a look around the room. Even after being there for a couple of hours, he hadn't noticed anything about her living room; and as he knew of old; how a house was told a lot about its occupier. This room was no exception; she was a mam first and foremost! There were pictures of her little boy everywhere; from being a first born to what must be the most recent as he was in a little uniform and the photograph hadn't actually made it into a frame. There was also every age in between! There were toys everywhere; but they were all stacked in neat piles and the room was clean and tidy! Very like its owner! Nichola was fun; but she also took care of herself. There was no sign of Mr Jones anywhere and as if she had read his mind; Nichola filled him in on her situation!

There had been a Mr Jones, but they split up a few months ago and he was currently back living with his mam while they decided if the separation was a permanent thing or just a little blip in their relationship.

Mr Jones had lost his job around the same time as Mrs Jones had found out she was pregnant. The timing had been terrible and although seemingly Mr Jones had severable employable skills; no job had materialised and Nichola had worked full time for as long as possible at Pearson's, took as little time off when she had Seth; the little boy and returned to work in the knowledge that Mr Jones would be Seth's main carer. She didn't know if she resented Mr Jones having Seth more than she did or that he seemed to have given up altogether, so she dropped her hours to part time in the hope that the depleted income would spur her husband on to get a job and allow them to live some kind of normal life.

No job had materialised; there had always been an excuse as why not to apply; the money was so tight that it just put too much strain on their own relationship and she asked him to move out. He was working now; but although they spent time together; she wasn't sure if they could ever get back to where they were; and she wasn't sure if she wanted to! Let down was a word she used a lot as she recited her eulogy about the absent Mr Jones to Mack!

Feeling the need to 'share'; he told her a little bit about his relationship with Carly. He obviously missed out all of the bits about his serial cheating and his eventual downfall. But he did tell her that she had been the only girl he had ever lived with and how it still upset him sometimes that he wasn't with her and that seeing her with someone else had felt like a kick in the teeth! It was basically true; omitting the fact that he couldn't keep it in his pants was just an oversight!

(28) ME AND MRS JONES   #michaelbuble

Nichola Jones leant in and kissed him. He had seen it coming! If he was honest, he knew before he even rang her doorbell exactly what was going to happen, even if Mr Jones had been around; this was always going somewhere! He was kidding himself that he thought he was on safe ground; he knew exactly what sort of ground it was going to be.

It was the living room carpet with the lovely Nichola Jones on top of him. He didn't resist. He kissed her back! He did think that he didn't want to be the excuse for Nichola not getting back with her husband; the father of her child. But he now had a raging hard on and no amount of sensible thinking was going to stop him from putting that raging hard on between the lovely Nichola Jones legs!

He ended up staying the night. They had a lot of sex and it was just aswell there was no one else there; she was one of the noisiest women he had ever been with. She screamed she shouted and she had a mouth like a sewer. It was unexpected and a right turn on. She scratched and she bit! Not enough to 'hurt, hurt' him, but it certainly got him going!!

His body the next day was covered in little teeth mark and scratches. One thing was for sure; he couldn't be with anyone else for a few days; it was obvious what the marks were from!

It had turned out to be a good night; he was sleep deprived and a little sore when she let him out of her house very early the next morning. He needed to go home for a shower and change of clothes before he went into work, but there was the saving grace that the alcohol had long gone and he was safe to drive home without fear of being caught drink driving or totalling the truck!

He wasn't sure about what would happen next. He had been in the same situation many times; slept with a work colleague and then immediately regretted it when he saw them at work again. He had only been officially at Pearson's for a week and already he had had sex with two people there! A leopard couldn't change its spots; would he always take what was on offer?? Maybe he just hadn't met anyone who could be everything to him. One day his looks would fade so he may as well make hay while the sun shone!!

Mack arrived at work at exactly the same time as Nichola Jones. She looked over and waved; there was no flirty banter; no knowing looks. To his own surprise he didn't feel regret. He didn't feel the urge to go and hide in the toilets to avoid her. She hadn't text after he left saying what a good night she had had with him. Nothing! Me and Mrs Jones Mack thought to himself as he made his way up the pitch towards his office; he was going to sell his first car today; he could feel it in his bones!

(29) YOUV'E GOT A FRIEND IN ME   #randynewman

Mack's mam pulled her car up outside the pub where Justin and his girlfriend were having their housewarming that wasn't a housewarming. He had been just going to get a taxi, but Paula had offered and he had jumped at the chance; it had been two weeks since his last pay from the Call Centre and he still had another two to go until his first pay from Len Pearson Cars; and then it was only his basic so had to watch his money!

And it was nice spending a bit time with his mam. They were like ships passing in the night at the minute. When he was at the Call Centre he used to work earlies or lates so often had a morning with his mam when her shifts fell on the same as his. They would spend many a morning watching Jeremy Kyle eating toast and drinking tea; it was more often than not toe curling; but addictive! There for the Grace of God; his mam would say when someone failed a lie detector test or the DNA proved that someone else's cheating boyfriend was the father of a disgruntled mother's child!

But if gave them time together. They had always been close; there had always just been the two of them and as Mack got older; their relationship was based on friendship. They had a similar taste in music; his probably founded on his affinity with the Housemartins and his connection to their lead singer! But they liked to go and see bands live and when he was old enough; his mam would book them tickets and off the two of them would go! It was the same with sport; his mam loved football, so it was never a hardship for her to take him to St James Park and watch Newcastle United play!

They had holidayed abroad together and when he got a bit older she never minded him taking a friend with him. He had had a good childhood and whereas his mates had rebelled against their parents as they went into their teens; Mack had never felt the need. He hadn't been an angel by any means; but there had been no major dramas; just his lust for girls which his mam had recognised when he was very young and always tried to advice how not to behave! He might have been a shit; but he was a decent shit and didn't would go out of his way not to deliberately hurt anyone.

When he was growing up his mam had had boyfriends; he had met a few of them. If they were serious Mack would be shipped off to spend the weekend with his Nan and Granddad now and again. Not that that bothered him; he loved them. When he was small they were always around taking care of him while his mam worked, so the odd weekend staying at their house was always a treat!

They had been together forever; childhood sweethearts, after they retired they did everything together. They had a good life; that was why when his Nan died his Granddad fell to bits for a long time.

Mack had such good memories of those weekends. They would have a game of cards or Scrabble; he was an ace at Scrabble. He wasn't that good a spelling, but he had the happy knack of adding a tile here and there and making a double or treble word score. He would watch old DVD's with his Granddad; his Granddad loved all of the old seventies and eighties sit-coms, the likes of would never be screened in todays politically correct culture. And of course, there was endless hours of Minder and the Sweeney.

If his mam's boyfriend was a serious prospect, then Mack would be introduced. They all seemed to be ok; but he was always a bit suspicious of them. His mam was everything to him, he never wanted her to be sad. But inevitably relationships didn't always last and sometimes his mam was sad. He always felt bad about it and hoped that they didn't split up because of him; it was never talked about who spilt up with who. She would soon be back to normal though and the two of them trundled on together.

(30) LOCK UP YOUR DAUGHTERS #slade

When he moved in with Carly it gave his mam the freedom she had never had. Who would want to bring a bloke back when there was already a young alpha male in residence! He had taken the mick when she had joined an online dating site; but he had also been worried. She was a single female living alone. But Paula wasn't stupid; she had been on her own a long time and he knew she wouldn't take any risks, but still. He didn't need to worry though; she met Tom very quickly after joining; they just sort of clicked and now seemed to be a permanent fixture in her life.

That was how he had come to get a lift off his usual nervous of driving new places mam. It was one of Tom's daughter's 21st birthday and his mam had been invited to her party; she was his mam and he was biased; but she did look lovely and nowhere near her age. He hoped Tom appreciated just what he had in Paula! And Mack had been invited to meet Tom's girls the following day for lunch; something he milked all the way to the pub where Justin was having his housewarming party that wasn't a housewarming!

Thinking he was funny, he jumped out of his mam's car outside the pub and blew kisses at her as she drove away, knowing that even though she made out she was angry that he said he was going to seduce the daughters; she knew he wasn't serious. Or was he; he hadn't even set eyes on them; so he couldn't really say it would never happen!

Justin and his girlfriend; who Mack thought was called Amanda, had booked the upstairs room in the pub. He hadn't been in before and had no idea where he was supposed to be going and because his mam had been time bound he had arrived at the party earlier than he would normally have put in an appearance; so ordered a pint and stood at the bar.

It was quite busy; there had been a match on earlier in the day and there were a few people in wearing Newcastle United shirts and sprinkling of younger people who looked like they used the pub as a meeting place and would be heading off into the city centre for their evening entertainment. Mack didn't see anyone he knew so ordered another pint and stayed propping up the bar. If no one came in he knew he would be legless before he even made it to the party!

(31) RIDIN SOLO   #jasonderulo

He maybe should have brought someone with him; he hadn't thought. All the talk in the garage had been about the party, everyone seemed to be going; Justin was a popular lad and he was also a Pearson so no one liked to decline the offer, they wouldn't have liked to put Justin's nose out of joint. Len Pearson treat everyone who worked there like an extension of his family; that was if they weren't already a member. Any work do's were always a big thing there!

Although Mack had only been there two weeks; he felt very much part of the team. He had been right when he had said he was going to sell his first car on the first Saturday he had worked there; he had and another and over the course of the next week he had got another half a dozen under his belt. The garage had been busy and the cars were literally flying through the door. Everyone had helped him; whether it was closing a deal or delivering a car to one of his customers. There was always someone there to show him the way.

The lovely Mrs Jones had remained just that. She obviously wasn't a gossip; there had been no mention of their liaison and when there was an audience she behaved just as she had when she had first met him and flirted outrageously. But outside of work he hadn't heard from her; whether she felt guilty about cheating on the absent Mr Jones or maybe she just hadn't thought Mack worth a second go; his mobile remained Mrs Jones free; and somehow it irked him!

Only that morning he had thought about getting in touch with Melissa; he had deleted her number but her messages were still there and it wouldn't have taken much to work out which ones were from her. He had liked her; and for that reason he decided he would just let sleeping dog lies. That and the fact that even a week after his encounter with Mrs Jones; he still had bruises all over him; they might have faded to a horrible mauvy/yellowy colour; but there was no mistaking how he had got them and as sure as eggs were eggs; if he had met up with Melissa; he would have got naked with her.

So, he was flying solo. Mrs Jones was going to the party; he had heard them all talking about picking each other up when he was in the office. Did he fancy his chances with her again? He really didn't know! She didn't seem too keen on him and in typical Mack fashion, why didn't she? They had had a good night; she had enjoyed herself; he knew she had; he could spot a faker a mile off!

Just as he was about to order another pint, Mack felt someone come up beside him and start rubbing up and down his leg. Thinking that it was Mrs Jones doing her usual full on Mack flirtation thing in front of her friends; he spun around to be confronted by a laughing Craig Reed. He was with another lad who Craig introduced as Sean and by the way he was holding on to Craig; was his boyfriend.

(32) OUR HOUSE   #madness

Mack bought them drinks and Craig told them to follow him; he had been to a party at that pub before and knew where the function room was. Sean was carrying a present; Mack hadn't thought about it; he would buy Justin a card over the weekend and put £20 quid in and give it to him next week. It wasn't even a housewarming; it was in a pub, so he could be forgiven for not getting them a proper present.

But how wrong he was! As they pushed the door open into the function room; Mack couldn't believe what he saw! It looked like a flat! Whoever had done the decorating had done a really good job.

As they stepped in through the door; they were in a living room; it maybe had more settees than your average two up two down would have; but it was most definitely a living room. Tall partitions housed pictures and photographs of the happy couple; there was a flat screen television and on the far side there was a pair of curtains hanging off a pole; these were obviously closed but with the addition of lamps all around the room; it really did look like he had walked into someone's home!

It was absolutely mint!

There were already a few people there. Some were sitting on the settees; others were standing around the room in little groups. There were gaps around the room the size of a standard doorway; Mack follow a very excited Craig through the first door and into what appeared to be a kitchen/dining room which was doubling up as a bar. It was all so very authentic!

Justin was sitting at the dining room table with a few others; when he saw the new guests arrive he jumped up to greet them. Laughing he was telling them that he had been dying to tell them about the housewarming in the pub; that they had booked the room for the full previous week just so they could get everything ready in time. Then he was shouting for his girlfriend to come and meet his workmates. Craig had no doubt met her before because as soon as he saw her he was jumping up and down screaming and she seemed equally excited to see him. Amelia! Not Amanda.

Turned out Amelia worked in interior design and this was event was a dual function; the housewarming and a sort of marketing exercise. Mack had to admit that the whole thing was pretty awesome! Who would have thought it!

Thinking his mam would love all of it; he took out his mobile and started taking photos while Craig and Sean gave the hosts their gift; grateful that he could move away and not have to stand awkwardly not handing over to them a gift of his own!

Amelia had certainly gone all in. There was a kitchen clock; a sink; even a pedal bin! No detail had been spared. Mack made his way back into the living room which seemed to be more crowded than when he left; but still managed to get some good pictures of all the little features. Through another gap and he was in what appeared to be a spare bedroom; complete with matching twin beds and another set of drawn curtains along with bedside tables hosting little lamps and a bedside rug!

Back through the gap and along a little corridor and there was another little opening with a shadowy light shining out. This time is was the master bedroom; complete with four poster bed! Was there anything left in Amelia and Justin's flat?? Even if he was a bloke and not in the slightest bit namby pamby; he appreciated something when it looked good; and this bedroom looked good. It could be in the swankiest hotel in town. Everything screamed elegance! The lighting; the furnishing. It was the real deal and if it wasn't for the noise coming from the other rooms; he could have been anywhere.

Just about to step in and take some photos; he noticed that there was someone sitting at the dressing table brushing their hair. He stopped; she had obviously seen him long before he her; Elle Pearson.

(33) HELLO AGAIN   #neildiamond

Mack had thought she may be there, but three pints and a décor masterpiece later; he had forgotten all about her. And there she was; staring back at him in the reflection of the mirror; even in the dim lighting, he could see her amused look at his discomfort.

For once in his life; Mack panicked and instead of being a gentleman and speaking to her; he backed out of the room and made his way back to the living room where he could lose himself in the crowd and finish his pint.

Fuck, fuck fuck he thought to himself as he made his way over to one of the settees where Craig and Sean had plonked themselves along with some of the others he worked with. Sean was still kindly holding his half empty pint which Mack relieved him of and necked.

He wasn't used to not being in control of himself; and he really had thought she would be there; but to encounter her in an empty bedroom, even a pretend one; had been a shock. And she had looked stunning, from what he could make out of her anyway!

He went to the bar and bought drinks for him and his two little friends; the living room was quite raucous by the time he returned; everyone was in the process of pushing the settees around as the DJ who had been nowhere in sight when he left the room a few minutes earlier; struck up the lights and music on what he had assumed was a sideboard; yet another illusion, had that equipment been there all of the time??

Another pint gone and he was back off to the kitchen. His boss had arrived and was sitting where Justin had been sitting earlier. In fear of being too pissed to talk to him later, he made a beeline for him and was greeted by a warm handshake and a huge smile! Mack was introduced to Mrs Pearson, Laura!

She was much younger than Mack had first thought; he knew that she was Mrs Pearson No.4 but had just assumed she would be around her husband's age. Laura Pearson must have been almost half her husbands. She wasn't particularly good looking, but her laugh was infectious and the way she held on to her husbands' hand, she was obviously devoted.

They both made Mack feel very welcome, very much part of the work team and were looking forward to spending more time with them in the future. He turned to make off to the bar and walked straight into Elle Pearson! He had no option but to talk to her; how was she? Yes, he was fine thank you! Yes, loving the job so far! Yep, catch up later! For Mack and his usual confidence around women, he felt pathetic.

(34)   TORN BETWEEN TWO LOVERS   #marymagregor

More drinks ordered and again someone rubbing themselves up and down against him. Craig was a pest! But this time it wasn't Craig showing appreciation for Mack's firm thighs; this time it was Mrs Jones!

She was obviously a little bit pissed, because she didn't have any of her mates with her to show off in front of and she was still standing there looking at him seductively! She too looked stunning! And the way she was looking at him, Mack hadn't been the flop in the bedroom that her no contact impression had gave!

He was going to chat to her, when someone squashed into the bar next to him. He could smell her; he had noticed her perfume when he had his fumbled conversation with her a few minutes before. Elle Pearson. She didn't appear to be at a bar never mind pushing her way in, but it was her and the thought of striking up a flirty conversation with Mrs Jones in front of her seemed like a childish thing to do. So telling Mrs Jones he would see her in the living room; he made his way away from both of them!

It took will power for him not jut to neck his pint but being pissed was the last thing he needed to be; he needed to keep his wits about him. Two weeks in the job, two women; he was too weak!! And both of them looked hot! If push came to shove he didn't think he would be able to choose. Elle Pearson and her control versus Mrs Jones and the screaming and shouting; both equally appealing in their own right; both worthy of another, he would say go, but that sounded callous, but still!

He was torn between two women!

(35) GIRLS GIRLS GIRLS   #jay-z

Not that it hadn't happened before. It had happened lots of times at the Call Centre, he had slept with so many of them it was inevitable that they would be overlapping but even away from his workplace he had been to places where two or more of his conquests had been there at the same time.

The most memorable had been a house party. He had slept with one girl a few weeks earlier and another just the week before. Not that it bothered Mack, he wasn't having a relationship with either of them and hadn't led them to think otherwise. But the drink had flowed and the first girl was there and then they were heading up the stairs and into one of the empty bedrooms. The second girl hadn't been happy. She had seen them going up the stairs and knew what was going to happen. So, she had followed them; went into the bedroom and joined in!

And that had been Mack's first threesome. It had been that simple. Neither girl had held back; with him or each other; it was the stuff porn films were made of and Mack would never forget it. You never forgot your first time!

He couldn't imagine Mrs Jones and Elle Pearson getting it on; they were Ying and Yang; one cool and controlled and the other frantic and a little bit feral, but what an experience that would be!

One thing was for sure; Mack couldn't stay at the party. The only way he could handle it was to drink and if he got drunk God knows what would happen and he had only just got his job. Two women was far too risky.

He found Justin and thanked him for inviting him then made a quiet exit. Taking his mobile out of his pocket he was about to look for a taxi number when he saw he had a message from an unknown number. He had Mrs Jones number so it could only be Elle Pearson. Fuck, fuck and infinity fuck Mack thought. Had Mrs Jones blabbed?? He didn't even know who Elle Pearson had come to the party with. There had been quite a party of Pearsons around the dining table. Did she even have anyone?? Boyfriend? Husband?? Even in the two weeks that he had worked for her dad there had been no mention of her, not even off blabbermouth John Rippon. And he hadn't asked.

Outside the pub he opened the message. How's the new job going?? Do you fancy a catch up?? I've missed you! M x

Melissa!!! What a fucking relief! Horned up with the two hot women at the housewarming that wasn't a housewarming which actually was quite like a housewarming, he replied back, told her where he was and did she want to pick him up and they would could have a catch up!! Within minutes she had text back to say she would be 30 minutes. He didn't want to go back in to the party so went and sat at a nearby bus stop! He would think of something to talk his way out of the bruising all over his body! Maybe he could have got them sparring in the gym!

Whatever; one thing was for sure, sweet Melissa would be getting more than a catch up when he caught up with her!! He had given her up to the God's of Fate and they had returned her; on any other night would he have replied; perhaps not; but she was just what he needed right there right now; tomorrow was a new day!

(36) LET'S GET IT ON #marvingaye

The weekend of the party had turned out to be far better than he could have imagined.

Melissa was really nice. She may have been in the right place at the right time but he had no regrets about hooking up with her again. She had picked him up outside the pub and they had drove back across town and went for a curry and of course a catch up.

It was nice to hear all the gossip about what was going on at the Call Centre with his former colleagues. If she had been pissed off about him not being in touch in the intervening two weeks; she never said. She looked really pretty sitting across the table from him; he was a little bit drunk, but he knew sweetness when he saw it! Very different to the two women he had abandoned at the housewarming party; he soon put them to the back of his mind and gave his full attention to Melissa!

There were no awkward silences; the chatter flowed. She was as interested in his job as he was in hers and before they knew it the meal was eaten and they were finishing off their drinks. They hadn't spoken about what would happen next; but the twitching in his Calvin Klein boxer shorts was becoming less of a twitch and more of a banging on the zip to be out; he had to get her out of there before walking out of the restaurant became something of a spectacle!

They left and without saying anything they were in her little car and heading back towards her house. It was in darkness, but Mack knew her parents were home; an element of restraint was called for. But they were barely in the front door before he had a hold of her and his hands were under her jumper and fingers were pinching her nipples. His mouth was over hers; she may not have been Mrs Jones; but he didn't want her mam and dad trotting down the stairs to see what the commotion was all about!

She pulled herself away, pulled him into the kitchen and pulled her jeans and her knickers down. With her sitting on the kitchen bench, in the dark Mack showed her how much he had missed her the past couple of weeks! But the drink and dark disorientated him a little bit and as he took her to climax; images of Mrs Jones and Elle Pearson flooded his mind; that and a little ménage et toi he had participated in years early. Just as she started to shudder; he had his hard on out and into the Melissa's sweet spot! He didn't last long, but it didn't matter, he would do it again. One thing that he never suffered from was brewer's droop; on many occasions it had the opposite effect, and he couldn't quite reach where he needed to be. But not that night; his appetite had no bounds and when they both eventually fell into Melissa's bed; it was an exhausted satisfied sleep he entered.

They probably slept longer than they intended. It was late morning and Mack had a Sunday lunch he needed to be at or woe be tide him; his mam would be furious. He hated having to do it; but it was out of bed and virtually straight into Melissa's car, he knew her mam and dad were around the house somewhere, but he really didn't have time to meet them; not that Sunday morning anyway. He sort of felt guilty; Melissa was sweet and because of his lust for sex he had reeled her back in again. They hadn't seen each other for a couple of weeks; it would have been easy for him to just leave it and let her get on with her life, just as he was his. But his twitch had caused the text and the rest was history.

This time when she dropped him off, he didn't offer her back to the Gods; his conscience wouldn't allow him to and he arranged to see her through the week and maybe they could go to the pictures or something! To his surprise he found he didn't mind; she was good company; a bit of a looker and the sex was getting better each time; she wasn't half as timid as she had been. No seeing Melissa again would be no hardship!

(37) BEST FRIEND   #50cent

Sunday lunch turned out to be really good. His mam again looked lovely; she scrubbed up well. And she seemed really fond of Tom and he of her; maybe this was something special; Mack hoped so, it was about time his mam had someone to look after her. It was Tom's youngest daughter Lucy's 21st! she was there with her boyfriend who looked about 15 and Lucy didn't look much older; or maybe it was just Mack getting old! The other daughter Becky looked about Mack's age; though could have been 45 if she shared her sister's youthful genes!

But they were nice; and made Mack as the stranger of the group feel very welcome. Lucy was at University and much to Mack's delight Becky worked for Newcastle United; how hadn't his mam mentioned this to him before?? Becky was Mack's new best friend!! Becky didn't just work for them, she proper worked for them; she was a physio; she actually worked with the footballers. Before they had finished their main courses; Becky had promised Mack she would get her new 'step-brother' tickets for the up and coming cup game. Result!! He avoided eye contact with his mam; he didn't want to see the 'don't you dare look!'

Back at work on Monday morning, all the talk was of Justin's Housewarming that wasn't a housewarming! Mack had bought a belated card and shoved a few quid in; he had felt like an idiot for not giving him a gift on Saturday! The party had trundled on until midnight and then a huge group of them had went on nightclubbing! By the looks of young Craig; he was still suffering. But Mack had no regrets about not staying at the party; he had avoided any drama; for now, anyway!

Work was busy; he was going away on some type of course the following week so had that to sort out and because there had been a bit of a cold snap weather wise; the garage was busy busy with customers looking for a more reliable car!

Mack took a call from someone called Jenny who was looking for a specific type of car. He knew they had a couple in stock so directed her to the website where she could see photographs of them. The rule seemed to be if you made first contact then it was that salesman's customer and if it progressed to a sale then they got the commission. On the pitch; it worked on a rota base; Mack as it stood took the customer if the rest of the team were busy. They had all been busy with customers so that how he had been able to talk to Jenny.

She called back asking for Mack and so he made arrangements for one of the cars she had seen to be taken off the pitch and prepared for a test drive later in the day. It was going to be a late finish for him; she wouldn't be at the garage until around 6 o'clock when she finished work; he didn't mind, he had nothing else planned for the night and he liked the thought of earning himself a bit more commission.

The rest of the day flew by; he had cars to hand over to customers who had bought them at the weekend and there was a steady stream of customers arriving at the garage. Before Jenny even arrived he had 3 sales under his belt and the garage as a whole had sold 11 cars; which was really good for that early in the week; bad weather certainly equalled sales!

(38) JENNY FROM THE BLOCK   #jenniferlopez

Jenny Coates arrived at the garage driving a Mercedes. Mack hadn't been expecting that and he certainly hadn't been expecting the likes of Jenny Coates. She was fit; by far the best-looking customer he had dealt with since joining Len Pearson Cars. Knowing of old that if he fancied someone he set of some silent siren that he couldn't hear but was obvious to the opposite sex; he did what he always did when he was under pressure and didn't want to set the sirens off; he thought of his Nan!

Not his Nan as a woman; that would just be weird; weirder than the siren. But his Nan and her values and beliefs. She had only been with his Granddad her whole life; she hadn't even looked at another man. His mam had always said that his Nan and Granddad were lucky; they had been perfect for each other and luckily had found each other when they were still basically children. But his Nan had no time for people who as she would say 'put it about'! in her day she said there was none of this 'try before you buy!' She always said if you made your bed; you lay in it! When Mack's mam and dad had got pregnant; his Nan had taken it badly; she took things even worse when they split. But as any good mother would do; she rallied and did everything she could for her grandson. When he was older; she would often view her opinions about women on the television or people they knew who as she liked to say 'had loose morals'!

So, if Mack found himself lusting at an inappropriate moment; like at the doctors or dentist or if he had thought about it in a situation like his interview with Elle Pearson; then he would conjure up his Nan in his head and think what she would say if he encouraged inappropriate behaviour and that would normally be enough to damped his amour!

He was all business like with Jenny Coates. He went through all the options for purchasing a car with her before taking her out and showing her the little Fiat 500 she had chosen over the telephone earlier in the day. She didn't like it. She wasn't rude or anything just said she didn't think it was going to be the right car; they then spent the next 30 minutes or so wandering around the pitch looking at the alternatives.

She finally settled on an Audi and wanted a test drive. It was now after hours and the majority of the garage was closed; there was only John and a couple of the office staff left. It would have been an hour-long job just to get the car out. she said she would be happy returning the next night.

And that was that she was off!

(39) WHAT'S MY NAME   #rihanna

Mack wasn't despondent; there may still be a sale to be had. He told John what was going on and asked to have the car made ready for the following night.

Did he want a pint with John??

He refused saying that he had something to do on his way home. He really didn't want an hour of gossip about Len Pearson and co; it had been a busy day and all he wanted was his tea and a long bath!

He didn't sleep well. He woke up in a cold sweat a few times; there seemed to be a lot of women in his dreams; Carly; Melissa and when he woke in the morning and tried to recall what had disturbed his sleep; he was sure Jenny Coates was in there too!!

The next day was much of the same; the only difference was that he had a lot of involvement with the lovely Mrs Jones; it was all of the paperwork! She was all flirty again; there had been no contact since he had stayed the night with her; but she had most definitely upped her game again; even if there was just the two of them she was all touchy! He didn't mind; he liked her and it wasn't going to kill him having a bit banter with her!

Just after 6 o'clock Jenny Coates arrived again. She looked and smelt even nicer than the night before. This time she loved the car and was keen to have her test drive. As was company policy; the salesmen drove the car out and if the customer wanted to have a drive; they would drive it back. Trade plate in hand they jumped into the car and headed out.

The traffic was still quite busy so it took a while even to get out of the garage and down the street. Jenny Coates didn't say much. She fiddled with the radio and moved the seat backwards and forward. There was an industrial estate about half a mile away from the garage and it was usual for the test drives to head there. Mack chatted about the car's miles per gallon, road tax etc; spewing out all the information he had gleaned about the car prior to her arrival.

Safely at the industrial estate; he pulled the Audi over and asked if she would like to drive the car back. She agreed to and they swapped places.

As they walked around the car to swap seats Mack gave her a quick once over! Nice! He wasn't good at guessing women's ages, if he said that Jenny Coates was 40 he would be being generous; she was probably older. But she obviously looked after herself and Mack appreciated a woman of any age who still cared about their appearance!

After moving the seat and adjusting the mirror; they were off. As they headed off Jenny Coates skirt started to ride up as she moved her leg on the clutch. And as she moved around the industrial estate's roads; testing the brakes and turning the corners; it continued to lift until there was a clear view of her stocking tops. Mack was trying his hardest not to look; he stared out of the window into the darkness and started chanting in his Nan's name in his head; Nan; Nan oh na-na what's my name? oh na-na what's my name? What was his name?? His Nan seemed to have been replaced by the sultry Rhianna and her na-na song!!

Fuck, Fuck, Fuck, the silent siren!!!!

(40) FAST CAR   #traceychapman

He wasn't concentrating what was going on and hadn't noticed that Jenny Coates had pulled the car over at the kerb and was looking at him. If she had been talking he hadn't heard a word!! He looked at her but not without at first glancing at her legs and seeing that her stocking tops were still on show! He knew by the way she smirked at him she had seen him look. Could she reverse the car around the corner? Of course he replied regaining his composure. But it was only momentarily and as she turned herself to reverse; he was lost on her legs again and those lacy stocking tops!

She was around the corner and reversing up into the cul-de-sac. He had no idea at which part of the industrial estate they were. He wasn't familiar with it in the first place and his lack on concentration hadn't helped. Once she was safely around; she stopped the car and pulled on the handbrake. He asked her what she thought of the car, she loved it, said she would sign the paperwork when they got back to the garage!

Thinking that was that, he didn't expect her to push the drivers seat back and basically push her skirt up so far that he could see the bare flesh of the tops of her legs in the dim light of the dashboard!

Mack was under no illusion where this test drive was going! Knowing what was now going on he was a goner! One look and a small smile and his hand was over stroking the lace of her stocking tops and his lips were all over her mouth! He wasn't arsed that she was older than him; there had been lots much older. He wasn't bothered that they were in a sale car on a test drive parked in a public place. All he knew was that he had a raging hard on and he had to have Jenny Coates!

He had no idea how long they had been as they pulled back up at the garage. An hour maybe. There had been no rush once they started; he kissed her for a very long time; first her lips, then her neck, then her tits paying special attention to her nipples which her the size of football studs. And then it was that bit of bare flesh between her stocking tops and her knickers; the softest skin part. But it was not as sweet as the place his tongue found! And when she was done; she did him. She knew what she was doing; they didn't have sex; they didn't need to they had mouths that worked!

(41) SIGNED SEALED DELIVERED #steviewonder

She followed him into the garage; first stopping at the loo; it was almost 7.30 and there was only John left. He looked relived when Mack went back into the sales office; maybe he thought his new salesman had crashed!!

To look at Jenny Coates as she came to sit down at his desk; you couldn't tell that she had just been romping in a car like a teenager. She chatted to John about the Audi and as Mack filled out the order form he heard her say that Mack had been very helpful and knowledgeable; he nearly swallowed his pen top!

She happily signed the order form; paid her deposit. As Mack tidied his desk he had to admit he'd had a very good night. John was still chatting to Jenny Coates; by the tone of his voice he obviously was in agreement with Mack's opinion and that she was a very attractive woman; if only he knew what had happened on the test drive he thought to himself. Mack could still taste her on his lips and the smell of her was all over him!

He walked her out to her car. They chatted about the Audi which turned out to be a present for her daughter's 17th Birthday; lucky girl Mack thought; it was almost new and although just small; it was top of the range and all singing and dancing. As she got to her car she turned and put her hand out for him to shake. He wanted to kiss her; the thing that happened on the test drive and her buying a car really didn't warrant anything less. But there were cameras everywhere and John was mooching about locking up the garage; so he took her hand and shook and gently rubbed his thumb along her hand.

As she jumped into the driver's seat Mack went to close the door. 'A friend of mine recommended you! She said starting up the car! 'She said that you would look after me!' Mack didn't have a clue, he had sold some cars, but didn't think he had made that much of an impression on anyone so they would recommend him by name! she must have seen the look of puzzlement on his face. She took hold of the door handle and started to close it herself! 'Elle Pearson, she said you were good! I've certainly got no complaints!' Then the door was closed and she was reversing out of the parking bay and away! Mack just stood and watched!!!

(42) SHOCKED #kylieminogue

Mack was flabbergasted.

The fucking cheek of it. It was obvious what Elle Pearson had said to Jenny Coates and it had nothing to do with his selling skills! She may well have wanted a car; but she must have had exceptionally good hearing to be able to hear his siren; or Elle Pearson had told her all about his interview with her!

He also didn't need to be set up with women; he had always done very well just on his own; thank you very much! And he certainly didn't need a 5-star trip advisor review off Elle Pearson. Even if the whole thing had been a coincidence and the thing on the test drive was purely due to Mack's inability to keep his eyes away from Jenny Coate's stocking tops; whatever the reason; Elle Pearson's involvement gave him an uneasy feeling!

It hadn't mattered so much at the Call Centre; he may have upset a few of the females there with his leaping from one to another; but he would never had lost his job because of it. It was different at Len Pearson Cars; the boss's daughter; her friend; the finance administrator; who next?? He already loved the job; he liked the people he worked with, the buzz around the place and of course his shiny truck. That could all be in gone in one wrong word; that's all it would take; one little snippet of gossip by any one of the women and the whole thing would be in jeopardy!

Mack needed to get a grip; there were plenty of women around without him having to do it right under his bosses' noses!

And just like any decent human being would do under similar circumstance with the smell of his most recent conquest all over him; he rang his booty call and arranged to see her the following night. He really liked Melissa; not like liked; there was no happy ever after driving off into the sunset together in his shiny truck; but he needed to build a wall around himself and if there was anyone who he wouldn't mind being covered by; it was Melissa!

That was Mack's thinking anyway.

But the following morning he thought it was all in vain when a message came from Len Pearson asking him to go and see him. Fuck Mack thought. It was his third week working there and he had never been summoned before; there was something wrong! John was missing; he hadn't come in first thing, no one said anything about his absence, but it hadn't happened before and that added to Mack's anxiety about his up and coming meeting!

(43) IT WASN'T ME   #shaggy

What if something had been said about the test drive? Had something been left in the car; there had been no items of clothing removed so it wasn't a stray pair of knickers. But what if there had been a tell-tale sign left on the upholstery?? What if someone had seen the car parked up in the cul-de-sac on the industrial estate; they hadn't exactly been watching out for anyone watching them! What if it had been a notorious dogging spot?? The what ifs went around and around his head.

In the end he decided that he may as well go and get it over with before he gave himself a heart attack.

Passing the finance office; Mrs Jones shouted of him! He couldn't hear what she said so made his way in. 'I was just shouting morning handsome!' she laughed. Not her blabbing about what they had done then he thought to himself as he shouted morning back to her!

This was ridiculous he thought to himself; he needed to stop being ruled by his dick! If he lost his job, he really couldn't complain. He couldn't exactly appeal for some type of leniency or go to his trade union which didn't exist. He would just have to take it and move on; maybe with the tiny bit of car sales he had learned he could get another job in the trade. But it would more than likely be another call centre; the handful of sales he had managed to convert was nothing in comparison to the years and years and years of experience in scripted telephone calls! He felt sick to his stomach!

Len Pearson was sitting behind his desk in his office. He seemed chipper enough as he told Mack to sit down. He was typing something on his laptop as only a person of a certain age can do; long and laboriously! It reminded Mack of his Granddad and how he sat for an age at his PC; for someone as young Mack he really didn't get it!

As slow as his Granddad was and considering how painstakingly he was just sending an email or checking a website; he still managed to cause himself mayhem and would be on the phone asking for one of them to go over and sort the dammed machine out; it was the same with his mobile; television; heating!! Anything that wasn't a relic from his youth seemed to pose a problem for him! He was of the generation that watched the first man walk on the moon; even now his Granddad was certain that the whole thing was faked by those bloody Americans; watching the footage Mack was somewhat in agreement!

When Len Pearson had finished whatever it was he was doing; he turned to give his visitor his full attention. This is it Mack thought to himself; his indiscretions outed and Mack shown out of the door! Though he could feel Len staring at him; Mack couldn't bear to look him in the eye!

'Just wanted a little chat Mack; you've been here a few weeks now and I havn't had chance to say welcome!' He went on to say that he had been pleased with what he had seen of the new starter so far; and that he seemed to have fitted in well with the rest of the staff. He chatted on and on! There was no mention of Mack shagging Len Pearson's daughter; or Mrs Jones in finance or Jenny Coates the customer! Mack had been biting so hard on his lip he could actually taste blood! He felt like a cat with nine lives and somehow, he had managed to land on his feet even though he had fallen from a very high height; in Mack's mind anyway!

Mack thanked his boss for the opportunity and genuinely told him that so far he was loving the job!

The rest of the meeting was about the course Mack was going on the following week. It was a new finance company that Pearson's were going to be working with. Initially it had been Mack, John and Craig going; but John had an unexpected appointment the following week so had gone a week early; hence his absence from the garage until Saturday! So, Nick would be going next week in his place!

Mack hadn't really given next week's jaunt much thought. He had assumed someone would be driving down, but it was on the South coast so were flying down on Tuesday morning and would be coming back on Friday afternoon! It all seemed very exciting; he had only ever been as far as the conference room for courses when he worked at the Call Centre!

And it was with a spring in his step that Mack made his way back to the sales office and the rest of his day!

(44) DIRTY TALK   #wyntergordon

Which ended much better than it had begun. He didn't make any sales but had a few good leads for later in the week and had managed to get the sales he had already done packaged off and the cars all sorted and sent to the prep centre.

With John away there had been a canny amount of banter in the office. Not that John stopped them having a laugh and a joke; he was just all seeing and all hearing. The other two actually called him the Oracle; obviously not to his face, but little got past him; good or bad!

Kevin was relishing Mack's trip away with Craig; if ever Mack had a son and he turned out to be gay, he hoped that he would have an outlook similar to Kevin's. He said it had lots of benefits; there would be no young girl's dad banging on the door accusing Craig of getting his daughter pregnant, Craig loved housework, cooking and would happily go shopping for hours and hours with his mam letting Kevin off the hook from a dismal day spent following his Mrs around the town! Mack loved it!

Every possible scenario was played out by Kevin and Justin; Craig getting into the shower with Mack; waking up in the same bed; mile high club …. They were relentless in their pursuit of putting Mack under pressure! He took it all and even added a few little role plays of his own! He was comfortable enough in his sexuality to know that young Craig was no threat; he was a nice kid though and from what learned about him so far; he liked him a lot!

Wednesday night was date night with Melissa. They had intended to go to the pictures, but in the truck Melissa had gone through the listings and there wasn't really anything on they fancied! There was a Groupon Voucher available for a steak night for two at a pub not too far away; it seemed like a good idea; Mack hadn't eaten much and had skipped tea altogether because he thought he would be having nachos and popcorn at the flicks!

So, they headed off and were shortly ushered to a cosy table for two; to be honest it was ideal and after such a roller coaster day at work; it was nice to just sit still! Two meal dates with Melissa in a week!! If she was getting the wrong idea about their relationship and Mack's intentions, he couldn't blame her! He had been such a twat over the past few weeks!

(45) INVISIBLE TOUCH   #genesis

When he was little he had a blanket; it went everywhere with him and he couldn't sleep without it; he didn't like it being washed and if his mam manged to get it off him and into the washing machine; he would play merry hell; it didn't smell right. As he got older, he no longer took it out with him; he wasn't one of those kids that took their teddy bear or dummy to school; on his first day of school he was far too grown up to bring along something from home. No he went to school without fuss knowing for certain that his blankey was safe under his pillow until he got back from school; or later when he went to bed!

His mam had wisely cut it up and made it into smaller squares; Mack thought she actually feared the day it went missing and would be lost forever. So there were about 8 smaller versions; he still had them in his sock drawer; all 8 of them. They weren't a nightly thing now; but if he was upset he would take one and it would spend the night or however many nights it was needed in Mack's bed with him!

Melissa was beginning to feel like a human comfort blanket! While he was with her there was no thought of Elle Pearson or Mrs Jones or Jenny Coates! The problem was that when he was with Elle Pearson or Mrs Jones or Jenny Coates; there was no thought of Melissa and that's where the problem lay!

Carly had been a comfort blanket for him! There had been no better feeling than falling asleep cuddling her in or waking up with their legs wrapped around each other; it was a safe place! But when he wasn't with her he was easily distracted and the thrill of the chase of another woman would be overwhelming and he would forget all about the safety that Carly was!

He never thought he was doing any harm, not really; Carly got the best of him. Or the best version of himself he could manage; even though he knew that he had been her everything; she had only been his everything when she was standing in front of him. Even if he was just in the bathroom; or she was in the kitchen and he was left alone in the living room watching the telly; he could easily be texting someone else. Unless he had physically shackled himself to Carly; there had been no hope; his attention would wander!

But he had wandered with the wrong person. He had worked with Jude Johnson; like so many other of his conquests; she was an operator at the Call Centre. Like others before her, Mack had got it on with her after one of the Friday Night Rituals to the local pub. She was a party girl and would normally be out all over the weekend so had never actually made it out with her workmates on a Friday night. The first time she had put in an appearance had been one Friday before payday and she had rocked up with one of the girls she worked with who had obviously paid her out!

(46) HEY JUDE   #thebeatles

Mack hadn't really had much to do with her at work; she worked in a different department and their paths hadn't crossed although he had seen her kicking about the building; he couldn't have missed her. She was pretty and she knew it! She seemed to have a permanent tan; and would wear bare midriff tops with jeans for work and didn't so much walk around the place; she more sashayed!

But she was fun and she brought a different dimension to the group who was out that Friday night. As was the norm; when some of the group moved on Mack was in the group and so was Jude! They ended up back at her flat and into her bed! It was good; as was through the day; at night she was confident and not shy about saying what and how she wanted Mack!

He only stayed an hour or so; he had Carly at home, but Jude seemed to be ok about him having a girlfriend and basically having to hump her and dump her! Jude was cool! And so began their little affair!

There was no reason for Mack to stray. Carly was an amazing girlfriend; she had been his best girl friend for so long they knew each other inside out. Maybe that was where the trouble was; there was no excitement anymore; the sex was beginning to be a bit predictable; it made him wonder how the likes of his Nan and Granddad had managed to stay faithful to each other for so long. But they were of a different generation. There was no excuse for Mack behaviour; and he had deserved everything that was coming to him!

Because the lack of excitement with Carly was made up for by Jude. The predictable became unpredictable and excuse the pun; Mack's dick loved it!

After the hour he spent with Jude he thought that would be that. But a few weeks later; the Friday before the next pay day; she was back at the Friday Night Ritual! He had only seen her a couple of times in the intervening weeks and that had only been in passing! This time they didn't follow on when the rest of the group moved on; this time they made straight for her flat and had the benefit of the extra hour or so before he headed home again!

She was certainly a girl who knew what she wanted and Mack liked the fact that she told him exactly what she wanted. A controlling woman was a woman after his own heart!

(47) LET'S TALK ABOUT SEX BABY   #salt-n-pepa

They exchanged mobile numbers and pretty soon after the second shag; they were texting each other. It was just sex; there was no chit chat; she would send him dirty texts at all hours of the day and night; he religiously hid his mobile out of sight; she wasn't shy in what she said and some days at work he would have to sit at his desk for fear of standing up and showing off his hard on for one and all to see! Then the pictures started to arrive!

She would take them anywhere; of everything!! Jude was reeling him in, and he was letting her! Until one afternoon she sent him a pussy shot and told him she was in the gents toilet! He was there in minutes; he was gagging for her. They had frantic sex in one of the men's cubicles and then she was gone. No niceties!

And that's how it continued. Jude would sometimes show up on a Friday night; sometimes she would just text him and tell him to go to her flat! She would be waiting for him wearing something mind blowing; basques; stockings and suspenders; and very very high heels! She was a little bit intoxicating and certainly addictive! The sneaky sessions at work continued; anywhere they could and his little car would often take some hammer if they happened to have their breaks at the same time! They were fearless!

Perhaps it would have continued on longer! As far as he could see Carly hadn't had any suspicions; as what happened when he was getting his end away somewhere else; he treat Carly like a princess. He would cook tea for her coming in from work; run her baths and when his affair with Jude was at its height; he suggested a holiday to Las Vegas! Guilty conscious!

But his up and coming trip to Vegas was something Jude wasn't happy about! On reflection she seemed to sulk when he told her he would be going away for a week; but it was just an instant and something that didn't faze him at the time! It obviously fazed Jude!

They never got to Vegas! Jude made sure they didn't!

(48) DANGEROUS WOMAN   #arianagrande

At the time he didn't think about it! He got a text from Jude telling him to go over to hers after the Friday Night Ritual. When he got there she was dressed up in a bra; tiny knickers; stockings, suspenders and some very high heels! She spent a long time tormenting him; he could look but not touch! As she touched herself she asked him to tell her what he wanted to do to her; he told her in the filthiest of vocabulary; all the time getting himself ready to carry out exactly what he said he would do! When she did give in and gave herself to him; it was rough and frantic and unlike anything he had ever done before!

When it was over she offered him a coffee; something she had never done before; but not wanting to appear to be a complete bastard and just go; he stayed. Jude asked about Vegas; when they were going? What they would be doing, where they would be going! Mack just chatted away; they were going the following Tuesday; they were obviously doing the casinos and if they could afford it pick up one of the shows; maybe a helicopter ride along the Grand Canyon. He should have noticed the cloudy look on Jude's face. He didn't! Not until afterwards, when he thought back; when it was all too late!

He should have known that Jude had become attached. She might have been a party animal and liked a good time; but underneath all the hair extensions; fake tan and fake eyelashes; she was just a girl. She was flesh and blood and although their relationship had been based on sex; they obviously had a connection; but a connection that went right over Mack's head in terms of what affect he was having on her! For him it was just a thrill; a dangerous game!

Mack didn't get chance to see Jude again before Vegas. He didn't even see her roaming the corridors at the Call Centre on the Monday he broke up; his mobile remained devoid of her name and he had no urge to call her; that would have been taking the piss out Carly; so he put all thoughts of Jude Johnson out of his mind and enjoyed the night before his holiday packing and messing around with Carly!

(49) VIVA LAS VEGAS   #elvispresley

They had Viva Las Vegas blasting out of the stereo on repeat and after closing the cases; Mack had a soak in the bath while Carly painted her nails sitting on the toilet talking to him! One minute they were a happy excited couple about to embark on a holiday of a life time; the next it was carnage!

Even now Mack felt sick at what happened; he was so ashamed. The long and the short of it was that Jude Johnson had filmed the thing that happened after the Friday Night Ritual. Warts and all! If he closed his eyes he can see as clear as day the look on Carly's face. Confusion; hurt then ultimate rage! He didn't have to watch it; he could hear every word! At first he had tried to deny it; say it had happened years ago; before him and Carly got together as a couple. But he had been playing 5-a-side football the previous Thursday and had taken a knock resulting in a black eye; the Mack in the video had an identical black eye!

He had been caught; hook line and sinker. Carly went absolutely berserk; she shouted and screamed and demanded the ins and outs; of course Mack lied and said it had been the only time he had been with the girl in the video. But Carly knew Mack; she had known him long enough to see right through him and his lies!

Then she was gone. Mack presumed to her mam's! She never returned. It was over; there was nothing he could have said or done to put it right. He called Jude but she didn't answer; he left her a vile voicemail and then got drunk sitting in-between the cases that would never see the light of day; Viva Las Vegas was still on repeat; for the first time ever; Mack cried over a girl! He had lost not only his girlfriend but his best friend! Jude Johnson and sexy underwear and her high heel never got a second thought!

If Melissa was his comfort blanket; even just a temporary one; he had to take good care of her. She didn't deserve to be hurt. With their meal finished; Mack didn't fancy leaving the pub; he didn't even fancy having sex; the little trip he had taken down memory lane didn't stir up any twitching; he was just happy to be in Melissa's company. Spotting something on the table behind Melissa; he asked her how her spelling was. Confused as to where the conversation was going; Mack jumped up and placed the box of Scrabble in front of them!

He had been sailing far too close to the wind. Wrapping himself up in Melissa would be a wise move; he vowed that he would settle himself down and see if things could work between the two of them. Even for a little while. She had the looks; she seemed to like him for who he was, and she was thrashing him at Scrabble; some things he would let her get away with; but beating him at Scrabble; never!

(50) GIRLS ON FILM   #duranduran

Mack and Melissa didn't have sex after Scrabble and it wasn't because she actually beat him over and over again. No; for once he was a complete gentleman and had taken her straight home and dropped her off. For whatever reason he just hadn't been in the mood; but they'd had a good night and arranged to meet up a few days later!

The rest of the week at work went well. Luckily for him; Jenny Coates was having her new car dropped off at home so he didn't have to face her and hopefully wouldn't need to see her ever again. Not that he hadn't had a good time with her; it had been mint; mind blowing. But her revelation about Elle Pearson recommending him had made him feel uneasy. It hadn't been all that long ago since Jude Johnson had tried to destroy his life; well less try and more almost did! He had managed to hold onto his job but that had been all. He had lost his girlfriend; his home and some of his self-respect when he had to go back to his mam's cap in hand.

He had a sneaky suspicion that Jade Johnson would still have that video tucked away somewhere; she didn't seem the type to leave things where they may one day be some use to her; though for the life of him he couldn't think of one single thing he could have that would be to her advantage. But still; he lived in dread that one day it would surface. At least now it was something from his past and couldn't do too much damage! Not like with Carly!

When it was very apparent that she wasn't coming back; Mack had packed up their home into plastic bags and boxes and text her to tell her to collect it all before he handed the keys back to the landlord. She had come when he was out; he never saw her again; apart from when he couldn't resist having a peep at her Facebook profile. Considering they had the same group of friends which they had shared together for years;

she was either very reclusive; or saw them when she knew Mack wasn't going to be there!

As for Jude Johnson, she was one person he wasn't sorry to see the back of when he left the Call Centre. The urge to punch her in her Botox mouth was unbearable, but that wasn't his way, he hadn't been brought up to disrespect women, not physically anyway; his loose morals had done their own amount of damage. No; he did something much worse to Jude Johnson; he went on as if he wasn't bothered. He had even managed the odd smile or two at her, much as it had irked him to do it! There was no way Mack would ever let Jude know the damage she had done. She never showed up again to the Friday Night Ritual and if she had tried to get in touch with him by phone; he would never know, she was blocked!

Jude and Carly were the greatest regrets in his life to date. For very different reasons of course, but the whole episode had left him shaken and stirred and that was one of the reasons his recent dabble with Elle Pearson and then Jenny Coates had set alarm bells ringing. He had no idea what those two women were all about! There would be no more scorned women; it just wasn't worth the aggravation.

(51) I MIGHT   #tomgrennan

Work was his priority. He concentrated on learning everything he could about cars and finance and the upsold products and the people he worked with at Len Pearson Cars! Never having been one keen on doing courses; he was even looking forward to his trip away the following week,

By the Saturday he had a couple of more sold cars under his belt and when he text Melissa to see what she fancied doing she told him just to go to hers! He really didn't fancy meeting the parents, as far as he was concerned it wasn't a meet the parents type of relationship; not yet anyway; nowhere near yet! When Mack and Carly broke up her mam and dad didn't speak to him; he didn't blame them. But it had hurt; they had always had a good relationship, even before he had become Carly's boyfriend and had just been her friend. Her dad was really cool and Mack loved being in his company like only a boy who had been brought up alone by his mam could understand. If Mack could have chose anyone in the whole wide world to be his dad; then Carly's dad would be it!

He wasn't a rocket scientist or anything; he was a gardener come handyman; worked for himself but worked hard and knew a lot of shit about a lot of shit. Even if he was busy, he had always made time for Mack. Losing that relationship had hurt Mack just as much as losing Carly had. But Carly's dad was one person he wouldn't want to run in to; Mack suspected that despite the good relationship they had had; he was likely to get his block knocked off for Mack hurting his daughter. No, the parent thing was most definitely something he hadn't intended to be entering into any time soon.

He was starting to like Melissa a lot; early days and he wasn't one for putting all his eggs into one basket, but the comforting blanket feeling he had when he was with her was starting to feel very comfortable indeed. Maybe having her properly in his life wouldn't be such a bad thing. He was a bit older and a lot lot wiser, he could give it a go, at least try to keep his pecker firmly in his pants; it was a thought!

Mack was never sure where his wandering eye had come from. Was it generic? On his mam's side of the family everyone seemed to be of the loyal type; his mam didn't seem to be one for jumping from relationship to relationship, he could count on one hand the amount of men she had been involved with; at least the ones he knew about anyway; then his Nan and Granddad had only ever had eyes for each other; his mam's brother, his Uncle Peter had married his childhood sweetheart Lynne and had been together ever since. So, it must have come from his dad; that was if it was generic!

(52) I WONDER WHO MY DADDY IS   #gregoryporter

He didn't really know much about his dad, Phillip. Only the bits he heard from his mam; sometimes his Uncle Peter told him about what they all to got up to when they were all at school together; even though his mam and Uncle Peter were almost a year apart; their birthdays had put them into the same school year, so everyone thought they were twins!

Phillip was always somewhat of an enigma. Obviously all the rest of the naughty things Mack had ever done were attributed to is dad; according to his mam anyway, but he never knew if his dad had been a womaniser or just a coward and a scaredy cat!

He did know that he had a younger sister; well half-sister anyway. He had found that out quite by chance; fluky really. He had been at a friend's birthday bash in Doncaster and she was there for her friend's hen party. Donny; at one point had been the go-to destination for everyone in Newcastle to go to for one of those special weekends. And as what always happened when Geordie's were away from their home town; they all sort of found each other and partied the night away together! Ironic really because if they had all been in Newcastle at the same time; chances were they wouldn't even speak never mind follow each other around on a huge pub crawl!

But that was how he happened to chance across Hannah! The birthday boys had met the Hens on the train on the way to Doncaster and arranged to sort of meet up later in the night after they had all booked into their hotels. It had been a riot of a night and loose arrangements had been made to meet up again the following afternoon before heading off on another bender on the Saturday night.

They had all been so drunk the previous night; they barely recognised each other in the pub the following afternoon. Luckily there had been no shenanigans between the two groups, just lots of banter and laughter which seemed to pick up where it left off and the night turned out to be as raucous as the one before.

Both groups were a mixed bag. In the 'hens' as well as the bride and bridesmaids; there was the bride's mam and an array of aunties and friends; as well as the mother of the groom and various friends of all ages and types. Then in Mack's group there were his mates and the birthday boy's dad and uncles and friends of the family; everyone seemed to have a mirror image in the opposite group. Hannah seemed to be Mack's!

(53) CALL ME MAYBE   #carlyraejepsen

He had spoken to her on the train; turned out she was the chief bridesmaid and seemed intent on keeping her flock in check and making sure everyone was where they needed to be and no one got left behind. She had her hands full; between the two large groups there was always someone at the toilet or somewhere else in the pub. She did it all with a smile on her face and as the weekend went on she seemed to seek Mack out to help her move everyone on.

Mack liked her immediately. She was like the clerk of the works and as they made their way between pubs and stuff; Hannah and Mack chatted away like they had known each other all of their lives. Turned out she worked at the airport for one of the big airlines; with being in front line customer service; she was used to moving people around and handling tipsy holidaymakers; and as it happened she didn't live far from Mack; they even had a couple of mutual friends. Small world!

Maybe if they both hadn't been sharing hotel rooms with others; Mack might have fancied his chances with her; she hadn't mentioned a boyfriend; not that a boyfriend ever stopped him; but there was no real opportunity for them to be alone and he didn't want to cause her any trouble. She was nice! And very good looking; brunette with sparkly blue eyes and lips that most women would die for; he hadn't felt them but to him they looked au natural!

As the last of them left the club in the early hours of the Sunday morning; they all said their goodbyes; they were travelling back at separate times in the morning. Mack did think of asking Hannah if she wanted to meet up when they got home; maybe she had the same idea because she asked him for his name so she could send him some of the photographs she had taken over the weekend to him. No problem; he didn't have anyone serious in his life so having a new Facebook friend wouldn't be a problem; no dramas! But as it turned out; it was!

Hannah Shearer! Of all the names in all of the world; she had one of the most famous surnames of all! The name was synonymous with Mack's home town. The legend who was Alan Shearer; Newcastle United and England hero. She obviously wasn't Alan Shearer's daughter, but she was someone's! And having a snoop through Hannah Shearer's Facebook profile Mack got a pretty good idea who was!

(54) TOON TOON BLACK & WHITE ARMY   #nufcfans

You see in his mam's box of very important documents contained his birth certificate. When he was born, and the future had been bright for the new little family; Mack had been given his dad's surname; it was there in black and white on his birth certificate. By the time he started nursery school; the name was a one Mack didn't even know; he was known only by the same name as his mam. There had been no Mack Shearer and no dad!

But later; when he was old enough to understand his mam told him all about his birth name being the same as his dad's and that she had changed his name to the same as hers; there had only been his birth certificate that couldn't be changed. He had never really thought about it much until he started to show an interest in football and in particular Newcastle United and thought there may have been a chance that Alan Shearer could have been his dad! Deep down he knew he wasn't; Mack had hair the colour of coal; his mam's was dark, but his was even darker; it was like a bluey black; that must have come from someone who with very dark hair; the famous Alan Shearer was fair. Nope the footballer wasn't his dad; it must have been like his mam had always said and it was that singer bloke!!

So the name Shearer crossing his path would always pique his curiosity! Hannah Shearer was no exception. She had sent him a friend request a few days after he got back from Doncaster; followed by a boat load of photographs from the weekend! She really was a very pretty girl and Mack wasted no time messaging her thanking her for the photos and asking if she fancied meeting up some time soon. While he waited for her to reply he took the opportunity of having a peep through her Facebook profile.

There were lots of profile pictures; as was typical 99.9% of all the females he was friends with on social media. If he said so himself; she looked very tasty in her airport uniform; she might not have been a trolley dolly, but she certainly had all the attributes to be a one! There were all the usual photos of her with friends and a woman he assumed was her mam and maybe little brother; there didn't seem to be a dad around; but the Shearer connection was as always a pull and he made his way to her friend list.

Four mutual friends; which wasn't surprising considering they only lived a few miles apart but what was surprising was the name Phil Shearer! Coincidence; possibly! It wasn't that much of a rare name; but Phil Shearer; Phillip Shearer! It was worth a look! So that's what he did; he clicked on the name and Newcastle United's logo opened up in front of him. Further delving was needed so he made his way through the illusive Phil Shearer's Facebook profile!

Within minutes Mack knew! This man was his dad! There were pictures of him next to a pool somewhere hot; building a snowman and lots of him on the terrace of Newcastle United. Shearer by name; Shearer by nature! Obviously, a massive Toon fan!

(55) PHOTOGRAPH   #edsheeran

Mack scanned through all the photographs; enlarging some of them to get a better look. He got where his mam came from when she had always said his dad looked like the lead singer of the Housemartins; there was a definite look there; but it was also clear where Mack's blue/black hair came from; not so much in the later photographs which seemed to be speckled with grey; but on the older photographs; Phil Shearer's hair was Mack's!

It was the most bizarre feeling! This bloke was his dad; there wasn't much information; he just seemed to upload photographs; maybe if they were Facebook friends he would be able to see more, but as much as he wanted to send a request; he wouldn't. Phillip Shearer had never bothered with him, so Mack would certainly not chase after him!

Back to Hannah Shearer; she was obviously a relation of Phillip Shearer's; because he was friends with her on Facebook now he could access all of her photographs and posts. It didn't take too long to find out how Hannah was related to Philip Shearer; he only had to scroll back a few dozen posts; back to the summer or more precisely to June! There it was; a picture of Hannah with Phillip Shearer! It was a nice photograph of them both; the post read 'Happy Father's Day to the Best Dad Ever!'

Mack felt sick! Especially just as he sat staring at the post a message popped through from Hannah answering his invitation of a meet up with a big fat yes! For fuck's sake! He couldn't believe it; it would have been bad enough if Phillip Shearer had been her uncle twice removed; but her Dad! Her dad was his dad! This whole thing was fucked up! But not quite as fucked up as it could have been. If she hadn't been so nice and so busy with the rest of the hen party; or even if they had managed to have some alone time; there was no doubt about it, they would have had sex! He could have shagged his own sister; the half was irrelevant; they had the same albeit diluted blood running through their bodies! Just having thoughts about what he had wanted to do with her turned his stomach!

He felt the whole situation was capable of pushing him over the edge. He needed to get a grip of himself and calm himself the fuck down! Realistically no harm had been done; he hadn't done anything with Hannah Shearer; he never had to see her again if he didn't want to; he could man up and tell her what he thought he knew; no more he could tell her what he knew; he was her half-brother. But that would mean a whole conversation with his mam about finding his dad and maybe having the man in his life and he wasn't sure how his mam would feel about that. He wasn't sure how he felt about that.

(56) CLEANING OUT MY CLOSET   #eminem

Phillip Shearer had never really been in Mack's life; he was a name and a face on an old photograph. He thought Hannah was about 3 or 4 years younger than him; which would mean that she was about when some of those photographs had been taken. His mam had never mentioned any other brothers or sisters he may have had, then on top of that he himself wasn't sure about how he felt about his ever-absent dad. If he was still in Hannah's life had he always been there? Was he still with her mam? Were there other siblings. Was the little boy in the photographs his brother too? Why hadn't he wanted to see Mack? There were just too many questions and far too many skeletons to be let out of closets!!

It was just too much. He wasn't even sure if he wanted Phillip Shearer in his life at all! He texted Hannah back and said he would see what shifts he was on and would get in touch with her soon! Apparently, she looked forward to hearing from him! Of course he didn't get back in touch; he couldn't do it! He couldn't see her and not tell her who he was! He couldn't go and meet her and pretend he didn't know who she was to him without having to tell her the truth; what if she came on to him; he couldn't knock her back without telling her the truth could he? Better the rejection now than later; let her think he was a complete twat now rather than later!

Mack kept his own counsel; he didn't say anything to anyone; Hannah never got back in touch; Twat – tick! Coward – Tick! Horrific situation avoided – tick! Reconciliation with Dad – not a chance! If Phillip Shearer somehow made his way into Mack's life it wouldn't be through Hannah!

The whole situation gave Mack the shivers; it still did. Hannah remained a Facebook friend; he often saw her on his newsfeed but always refrained from checking out her profile or engaging in any of her posts. He knew where she was if need be and if the day came that he ever needed a body part off a close relative; well he knew how to get in touch with his dad too! But that was as far as it went! For a long time Hannah Shearer stayed on his mind and for once it was a girl with a pretty face for very different reasons!

So where Mack's way with women came from remained a mystery; there was probably someone a few generations back that was exactly like him and somehow those genes had silently trickled through the generations until they reached Mack! Or maybe if was just his nature and it didn't come from anywhere! It was just him!

(57) GAMES   #demilovato

He really liked Melissa though; perhaps she was a keeper; she didn't have that thing that he really liked and kept him interested but it didn't mean he could coax it out of her! Time would tell.

So making his way to her house that Saturday night; he tried be positive about meeting her mam and dad; it was another step towards coupledom!

Melissa answered the door all dressed up! Confused he was sure she had said they were just staying in! Leading him into the living room; he expected to meet the parents; but the room was empty!! They were away for the weekend; they had the house to themselves!

And what a night they had! Melissa had food and drinks ready; not only that they were having a games night! Mack loved board games and it seemed Melissa had every board game imaginable! Not only that she had added an extra bit spice to make the night literally go with a bang! The girl was certainly catching on!

There was a little bowl for each of them! Who ever won a game got to pick a little piece of paper with a treat on it! Mack caught on quickly what it was all about and certainly wasn't going to play Monopoly; they started on Scrabble and the competition was fierce! It became very clear why Melissa was dressed up; she was properly kitted out underneath her dress in exactly what Mack liked best; stockings and suspenders!

Mack won a strip tease and a blow job in the first hour; but Melissa was better, she was the Scrabble queen and won herself a full body massage complete with essential oils, kissed in a place of her choice and 5 minutes of sex however she chose! He short-changed her on the sex; she maybe only got 2 and a half minutes; according to her anyway; Mack thought it much longer!

It was a good night; food, drinks and games; Melissa was beginning to come to the party and in his head Mack took another imaginary step towards him and Melissa becoming a couple! She was beginning to become something else and he was really enjoying himself with her

(58) LEAVING ON A JET PLANE   #johndenver

Then it was Tuesday and his mam was dropping him off at the airport; he still hadn't reached payday and money was too tight for a taxi or parking! He had money for expenses but when his mam offered he snapped her hand off! He was meeting the others there and they were going to have a quick drink before their flight; it was nine o'clock in the morning!

While he waited for the others to arrive; he sent Melissa a quick text telling her he looked forward to seeing her at the weekend! It was the truth, he was. He had stayed at Melissa's on Saturday night, and they had spent the majority of Sunday together; it appeared that her mam and dad had a caravan in the Lake District and spent a lot of weekends up there! He had swerved the parent trap for the time being at least! Hand on heart; Mack thought the more time he spent with Melissa and the more he got to know her the more he liked her!

Craig arrived giddy with excitement about their few days away together; he was a trier if nothing else; there was just Nick to arrive whoever that was. Mack assumed it was some member of office staff; there were a few he hadn't met yet or maybe someone out of the workshop; he hadn't thought to ask!

When Craig whooped, he knew Nick was there; Mack turned to see if he recognised the person from L Pearson's in the crowd. He recognised the person all right; Mrs Jones!!! How hadn't he made the connection. It hadn't been Nick; it had been Nic, Nicola! Then she was there standing in front of him; her hair down and bouncing around her shoulders; looking up at him she had the biggest grin on her face! That mouth!! That mouth with its shouting and screaming and biting! Fuck; something was stirring in his jeans! 'Oh Na Na What's my Name; Oh Na Na What's my Name ....

(59) Up Up and Away   #andywilliams

Mrs Jones obviously saw Mack's shock and openly laughed at him! At no point did he ever think that Nick was Nic and his little trip down to the south coast was with going to be with the delectable and somewhat dangerous Mrs Jones. Maybe dangerous wasn't the right word to describe her; she wasn't a Jude Johnson; he didn't think she would ever be out to cause him any trouble or embarrassment; but dangerous in the respect that up until the second she was standing in front of him; he had thought he had a chance of being a one woman man with Melissa!

Now he thought that prospect was very much in jeopardy! If it was just Mrs Jones at work; he could have coped. He could probably have coped with the odd works night out; but up close and personal, away from home. Staying in a hotel and her looking as hot as she did; he doubted it!

A couple of pints later and they were boarding the little plane. With Mrs Jones planted firmly in the middle of Craig and Mack; he was very aware of her leg pushing against his! Thank God it was just a short flight or joking aside; it wouldn't have been Craig and Mack joining the mile-high club! There was only one thing to do; earphones in, Rhianna playlist found and one specific song on repeat! Oh Na Na …..

The hotel was nice; it was right on the seafront and because he hadn't thought much about where he was going; he hadn't expected it to be a proper seaside resort; along with a pier and amusements! They had a meet and greet in the afternoon, but after that they were free to do as they choose; it looked like a fun place to have a night out in!

The finance company they were visiting was only a five-minute walk from the hotel; so after quickly changing into something a bit more office appropriate; they made their way there. There were about 15 candidates in all, and the afternoon passed quickly as they gathered in; somewhere that was no surprise to Mack; the conference room.

And then they were out and the three of them headed for the nearest bar that served food! The night turned out to be all right; Mrs Jones flirted tirelessly with Mack; but then so did Craig and it was good banter. Tiddly at the end of the night; they made their way back to their hotel and each to their own rooms! Mack was knackered; at the back of his mind he expected to hear a knock at the door or at the very least a text; but neither came and Mack slept soundly and alone in his own bed!!!! The delegates turned out to be a very lively bunch. The facilitators helped; one was as camp as Craig although he was old enough to be Craig's very young Granddad; the pair of them were like a double act and kept everyone amused; especially as some parts of the course were a little bit soul destroying.

Though the three of them were on the course together; they had been put into separate groups and he could hear Mrs Jones peeling with laughter; her being the only female in her group seemed to have turned up her velocity to a high; she seemed to be having a ball. It seemed that all the Geordies in the room were a hit!

The other course facilitator was a woman. She was older and Irish, and her voice stirred up some memories for Mack of a girl he had met on holiday. If he just listened to the woman's voice it could have been back in Ibiza with the girl whose name escaped him!

(60) Your My Best Friend   #queen

It had been a lads holiday; Mack's first. If he remembered rightly he was about 18 at the time; still young enough to be in touch with most of his school friends; and when one of them said did anyone fancy a week in Ibiza; a boat load of them booked on along with a few who would go out just for the weekend. In total there was about 14 of them wandering the bars of San Antonia that summer. It was everything a lads holiday should be. Copious amounts of alcohol; messing about and of course girls.

Because only one or two of them had serious girlfriends; it was a competition between the rest to see who could get with the most! Looking back, it was childish; but back in the day they were like young stags; full of swag and drink and no girl was off limits! It was literally a shagathon! And what a mixed bag they were! Some barely looked old enough to have even left school never mind legally drink; while others; like Mack and his best mate Marty looked to be already in their mid-twenties. They were tall, short, little, large; a right old box of teenage all sorts. Some of them Mack knew were just giving it large; but other like Marty would like nothing better than coming back with the title the 'Cock of the North' from Ibiza.

Marty was a looker. Only a couple of weeks older than Mack, they had found themselves sitting next to each other on the first day of nursery school and had been 'best mates' ever since. Like most lads they had fought and fell out over the years. They had on lots of occasions gone and found themselves new best friends; but they always somehow managed to make their way back to each other and to this day; Marty was always Mack's go to friend. They were M&M!

But back then; when their sexual prowess was at its height – it was game on in Ibiza!

They had been on holidays abroad together before; but usually with one of their families where their antics were curtailed. Ibiza was different. It was total freedom. They had booked apartments and there were four or five boys in each one; each apartment was next door to another one with friends in; it was a noisy affair!

Both tall and dark; where Mack was subtle charm; his Mack Attack was always under the radar with what Mack liked to think was a classy approach; Marty was full on!

No female was off limits to Marty. Each received the same attention as the girl previous to her no matter what she looked like. He just loved women. They came in all shapes and sizes; as long as they had a pulse, they were game for him. He was like it at home but in Ibiza; with the proximity of such a mass array of scantily clad women took Marty up another 20 notches!

Fun time around the pool; the drink flowed and the lilos were upended. Girls screamed that their make up and hair was being ruined; but nevertheless; minutes later the same girls would be floating past on their lilos again; teasing one of the Geordie Boys to jump in and tip them!

The boys were in their element.

(61) 5 6 7 8   #steps

After day one in Ibiza it was Marty and Mack one each. A few of the other lads claimed to have one conquest under their belt too. But it was game over. Marty would win! Mack had met Irish smiling eyes in the second pub they went to; she would be his one and only in the sunshine. Marty claimed to be in double figures by the time they boarded the plane back to Newcastle; Mack believed him. Marty was truly the Cock of the North! Mack didn't mind.

Irish eyes; which is how Mack would always remember her; had been singing on a little stage when the boys staggered into the bar. She was doing her own rendition of Nothing Compares to You with a full-on Irish lilt; Mack was mesmerised! Always one to appreciate people singing live; the girl most definitely had something about her, and Mack stood with his drink and watched her finish her set. By the time he made his way back to the boys they were ready to move on to the next pub; Mack felt a pang of disappointment that he hadn't had chance to tell the girl he had enjoyed her session; but there was drink to be had so off he went in pursuit of whatever the rest of the night had in store for him.

By the time dawn appeared most of the lads had gone; whether off with some girl or back to the apartments. Marty had disappeared; he had been last seen strutting his stuff on some dance floor, but Mack hadn't seen him for a good hour. For whatever reason Mack seemed to have drunk himself back sober; tired and hungry the last three standing headed back in the direction of their apartment block; their first day in Ibiza done; knackered and in need of their beds and if they happened to come across somewhere selling food; something to eat.

Luckily around the first corner was a little café; Mack wasn't sure if it had been open all night; or it was just opening up to do breakfasts; either way; the smell of coffee and bacon was far too good an opportunity to walk past; God knows when they would actually make it to breakfast if he went straight back; probably teatime. The other two dodged out; both a bit too drunk and the call of their beds was stronger than the call of their stomach; so, it was just Mack pulling out a chair and eyeing up what he could have off the menu!

The man that came out to serve him spoke English; as Mack ordered himself a full English with extras and a mug of coffee; the bloke chatted away asking Mack where he came from; how long he was staying and so on. Then he was gone, and Mack looked around to see if he could get his bearings in relation to getting back to the apartments! He would manage; he could just about see the sea; if he could make his way to the sea front, he knew he would find where they were staying! With the mug of coffee placed in front of him; he didn't take much notice of who brought him his breakfast until she spoke to him.

Irish eyes! Even though he had been quite drunk when he saw her in the late hours of the night before; he would have recognised her anywhere. Those eyes! They didn't speak beyond his thank you for the breakfast and he was too hungry to think of anything beyond clearing his plate and resisting the urge to lick the juice from his breakfast clean off.

He looked around to catch someone's attention to pay. The sun was already starting to have a bit of heat to it; and the earlier deserted street was beginning to come to life; but she must have been watching him because the next thing he knew she was sitting in front of him with two mugs of coffee and his bill!

In the cold light of the morning; she was still a bonny lass. She was as dark as he was, and she had the bluest of blue eyes; but whereas he was pale though at that moment tinged with pink from frolicking in the sun the previous day; she had olive skin which made her blue eyes even bluer. She sat and chatted as if she had known him for years. Turns out the bloke who worked at the café was her dad; and if he went to the loo and came back out through the opposite door; he would have been in the bar where he had heard her singing the night before.

(62) When Irish Eyes Are Smiling   #various

Her accent was very strong; even though they had lived in Spain for years; the girl had been back to Ireland for her education staying with her Gran and had only returned to Spain a couple of years ago. Mack didn't mention his age; she must have assumed that they were about the same age; 26 or 27 which made her quite a bit older than him!

They chatted until their cups were empty; he handed over the money for his breakfast, but as he was about to leave, she asked him if he knew his way back. Not one for missing out on an opportunity to spend time with a pretty face; he said he thought so; knowing that without a doubt he had made an impression on her and would take him where he needed to be!

And that she did! Via her family's beach hut where they stripped off and ran into the sea wearing only their underwear! Where in the sea they managed to have sex without removing the said underwear and then discarded it back in the beach house and got to know one and other a lot better!

Irish eyes had a mouth Mack could literally have died in! He wasn't sure if it was because she was a singer and was used to hitting the high notes; but God she was absolutely amazing – he didn't want it to end but because he felt that way; it did!

Walking back to his apartments he told her he would see her later; and he actually meant it! When Irish eyes are smiling the mouth does too!

So that was Mack for the entire holiday! Every night he would go to watch her sing; then in the early hours he would stumble his way back to the café and meet up with her there. The beach hut was their sex hideaway; and for the entirety of his holiday Mack swam every morning in the Mediterranean.

He did wonder if he was a one off or was it something she did all of the time; it didn't matter; he had a ball; if he was one of many or literally a one off; she did things to him he had never experienced up until that point. She was something else and although he couldn't remember her name; he would never ever ever forget her; those eyes; the hair; the body and that mouth of hers; singing or sucking; he loved it equally.

It didn't matter that he wasn't 'Cock of the North' – he didn't mind not having lots of shallow sex with a variety of girls; he had experienced something better! Mack couldn't remember if they had arranged to stay in touch; they hadn't, just like he knew they wouldn't. He couldn't even look for her on Facebook because he didn't know her name.

But years later two things happened. Marty went back to Ibiza with his then girlfriend. Irish eyes was still drawing in the crowds in her dad's pub. Marty didn't approach her; by that time Mack was just starting to see Carly so what would have been the point. But he did say that she did still look good! Mack would have expected nothing less!

And then the other thing was that not long after he moved in with Carly they were sitting watching the telly one Saturday night and he saw her. It was in the XFactor auditions; he didn't say anything to Carly; Irish eyes had happened years earlier; long before he and Carly had even contemplated becoming an item. But there she was standing in front of the judges; she was in her early 30's but he would have recognised her anywhere; those eyes; that mouth; that sound. It was sad to see that she was rejected by all of the judges; they said they liked her, but she was a bit too 'pub' singer for them. She was called Niamh! After all of those years Irish eyes had a had a name; Niamh; he may not have been able to spell it; but somehow Mack knew; he would never forget it!

(63) Hero   #enrique Iglesias

It was lunch break time back at the training course. For the life of him he couldn't remember anything about what they had been teaching for the past half hour or so; all he could hear in his head was 'Woah, we're going to Ibiza'! As everyone got themselves sorted to go to the nearest café for some food; Mack text his alter ego; the other half of the M&M duo; Marty!

They didn't see half as much of each other as they should. They still played 5 aside together on a regular basis; but beyond that there was none of the socialising there used to be; their relationship these days was based around texts and emojis! Marty had the perfect job; for him anyway. He was a fireman! It fitted his persona perfectly; played to his ego and was the best chat up line in the world! Women quite literally fell at his feet; he would scoop them up and devour them; but like his best mate; Marty had the tiniest of attention spans and there was always another damsel in distress for him to save!

And in career terms he seemed to be climbing the ladder; excuse the pun! Mack wasn't sure exactly what he did; but he had crew members now and seemed to have some authority about him. Having decided that he had wanted to be a fireman from a young age; it had been the only job he had ever done and therefore had all the privileges having any sort of longevity staying in one job gave you. He had a mortgage and a succession of brand-new cars along with a succession of girls to adorn them! But it hadn't been all good!

One of his best 'work friends' had died a year earlier; not through the job, he had some rare form of bone cancer and Marty had been by his side the whole way. It had made the usually upbeat Marty very insular and reclusive. For months there had been no girls; no going out; no doing anything beyond his job. Mack had been worried about him; he knew he had always questioned mortality; being a fireman he had faced death every day; if not the prospect of his own; then that of the people they went to save. Watching his friend die slowly in front of him had been something else!

Mack had gone to see him as much as he could; he didn't encourage him to go out drinking; that would have perhaps made a bad situation worse. But he did bully him into the weekly 5 aside football games; work commitments permitting, and he did try and at least text him every day. And then one day old Marty resurfaced; along with a new girlfriend who coincidently worked in the fire service but doing something desk bound! Whether it was because Marty decided life was too short and he wanted to leave his own impact on the world; or if Dina was genuinely who Marty had been looking for all of his life; but within months Dina was sharing Marty's home and pregnant with their first child!

Little Reggie had been born at the beginning of the year; much to Mack's amazement and Marty's joy; Dina was pregnant again already! Marty wasn't a new man; Mack had seen his roving eye still roving on many of occasions since he got with Dina; but he had taken to fatherhood like a duck to water; and Mack knew without a shadow of a doubt that Marty would never ever risk losing his baby boy over a bit of skirt. He had been there when Mack lost Carly! Marty was under no illusion that one wrong move with the wrong girl and the mat could well and truly be pulled from under his feet. If Dina wasn't the one, then she would be Marty's only one; for the foreseeable anyway!

Whether it was being away from home; or because Ibiza was fresh in his memory; Mack needed a catch up with his best mate; if Marty thought it strange Mack asking to see him as soon as; he didn't say. Just agreed to meet Mack on Friday when he got back from his training course! Mack felt ultimately better and even managed to keep his thoughts well and truly on what was going on around him for the rest of the afternoon!

(64) Black Magic   #Little Mix

The Len Pearson employees decided that they were just going to be holidaymakers for the night. The seaside resort was still bustling despite being out of season and the inclement weather; they ate fish and chips off a tray with a little wooden fork and they all had goes at the various arcades along the promenade; between them they even managed to win Mrs Jones's little one a Paw Patrol soft toy; she was over the moon!

When Craig and Mrs Jones let out a whoop of delight; Mack's heart sank. Fortune Teller! No way was he going in to be robbed face to face; and beside he didn't believe in all that mumbo jumbo; and said so very loudly to his two work colleagues who had sat themselves down in the chairs inside the tiny booth!

Leaving them to it; he set off on his own tour of the promenade; but on his own it didn't have the same appeal; he would feel stupid trying to hook a duck if he didn't have the other two at his side encouraging him. When the heavens opened, and the rain poured down he made his way back to the little booth and took the seat that Craig had vacated to go and get his crystal balls read!

For once chatty Mrs Jones was quiet. The little room was dark and morose and when they did talk it was in hushed tones. It was bizarre! Mack could hear all of the hustle and bustle of the funfair and arcades outside; but he couldn't hear a single word that was being spoken in the next room which only had a curtain as a door.

After what seemed like an eternity; Craig was out, and Mrs Jones was up off her seat and straight behind the curtain. 'Mack you have to go in! Madame Zeta Marie gave me specific instructions to tell you that she wanted to see you! She said tell your handsome boyfriend out there that he needs to come in and see what the future has in store for him! She said that Mack! I giggled because she had just told me where my future lay, and I said to her 'You've just told me who I'm going to marry and now your saying I have a chance for Mack to be my boyfriend! I want my money back!' Craig went on and on!

Mack didn't want to; he didn't have cash to waste on nonsense! Mrs Jones came out and he had no idea how it happened, but Mack was sat at a little table facing a woman he could only assume to be Madame Zeta Marie!

'Oh Na Na…..' Mack stopped himself. He didn't believe in being able to read fortunes or minds or cards or crystal balls; but just in case they could; he had better get thoughts of Madame Zeta Marie out of his head. He had been expecting some old gypsy type woman; he had looked at the scores of photographs outside the booth which showed a plethora of D List celebrities with Madame Zeta Marie; on some she was quite a young woman; the photographs mainly in black and white; in others she was older and in one or two; they didn't look like Madame Zeta Marie at all. There were certainly none of this version of Madame Zeta Marie who couldn't possibly have been a day older than Mack!

(65) China Girl   #david bowie

Regaining some control; Mack concentrated on what the lady was saying to him; her palm had already been crossed she said; his good friends had paid she said so all that remained for Mack to do was think of a question she would like him to answer! What sort of question Mack thought to himself!! Will Newcastle United ever win any silverware?? Will he be successful at his new career?? He didn't have a specific question to ask! She must have realised because she told him not to worry and hopefully, she would be able to pick up on something from him!

Madam Zeta Marie was pretty; no, she was beautiful. But she didn't look real. When Mack was little he would sometimes go and stay at his Auntie Lynne's and Uncle Peter's; while he was there his cousin Lou would show him her porcelain doll collection; Mack hated them. Each and every one of the dolls looked evil in his young mind; if he stayed the night he would always have one eye on the door in case his cousin's evil dolls took it upon themselves and made their way into his cousin Ryan's bedroom to murder Mack in his bed. He literally hated them; still did!

And that was what Madam Zeta Marie looked like; a porcelain doll. In the dim light her skin seemed to have a waxy glow; Mack was sure if he leant over and touched it it would be cold! She really was beautiful; but it made Mack feel uncomfortable; he just wanted to get out of the room and back to the hustle and bustle of the promenade! Any Na Na diminished the more time he was in her company!

Madam Zeta Marie was talking; someone was apparently standing behind him; someone who hadn't all that long been passed; someone he was very close to! It was the same someone who had been there since Mack and his friends had arrived; she had arrived; that was the reason for her insistence on seeing him! Gran she said! Mack was terrified; the urge to turnaround was overwhelming; the urge to run even more so! He couldn't hear what she was saying; she said something about taking his Gran's advice; but he had no idea what the advice was. He couldn't sit there a minute longer; she asked for him for his hand; she wanted to look at his palm; but Mack was having none of it. Without a backward glance he left; he could hear her calling 'Mack; Mack' after him. But there was no going back. Madam Zeta Marie and her talking to dead people wasn't for him!

Luckily for him; the other two were waiting for him outside the little booth; he took the opportunity to pull himself together before heading out to join them. Smile on face; he professed that the whole thing was a waste of time and their money; they laughed when he tried to give them a fiver back each for their trouble and insisted it had been their treat.

He needed a drink and remembering that he had seen a bar at the beginning of the promenade; he ushered the other two into its direction. With the refusal of them taking the money for Madame Zeta Marie's fee; he had no option but to get the drinks in; which at seaside resort prices was more than likely dearer than the reading. But halfway down the pint; his jangled nerves started to settle back into place!!

(66) I Want to Hold Your Hand   #thebeatles

Mack listened with interest while Craig recited almost word for word and accent enhanced; every minute detail of what the young fortune teller had to say. He had already it seemed met the love of his life; marriage was on the cards and he was going to be a daddy at some point in the not too distant future! The news made Craig even more giddy than Mack thought he could possibly be and before Mrs Jones had chance to recount her reading; Craig was off to call his boyfriend Sean and tell him of their up and coming nuptials!

And then there was just the two of them. Mack noticed that the moment Craig left; the usual chirpy Mrs Jones; was quiet and quite morose. Mack tried to tell her it was all rubbish; what could Madam Zeta Marie possibly know about their lives; it was all guess work; but Mrs Jones disagreed. She said she knew too much; even details; that couldn't possibly have been plucked from thin air. Mack didn't ask; if she wanted to tell him she would!

Craig text to say he was heading back to the hotel; he wanted to Skype Sean about their wedding! This made both Mack and Mrs Jones smile; he always went too far; but if Sean was singing off the same hymn sheet; there no doubt would be wedding bells ringing for them in the not too distance future. With nowhere else to be; they ordered another drink; and then another. Madame Zeta Marie seemed to have dampened both of their moods; a couple of drinks more seemed to make sense; Mack was tight on money; so ordered them a bottle of wine; the cheapest of all his options; but it wasn't until they were sipping on their first glass did he remember the last time he had shared a bottle of wine with the delectable Mrs Jones! Something stirred.

Mack knew he was on dangerous ground when they left the pub after demolishing the wine and the first thing tipsy Mrs Jones did was grab his hand. He didn't want to cause offence by pulling away; so held on to her hand as tightly as she was holding on to his. It felt good. He knew without a shadow of doubt that they were going to have sex again; he didn't want to be alone and neither did she!

Heading into another pub near their hotel; this time it was Mrs Jones who came teetering back from the bar with a bottle of wine and two glasses! By the time the bottle was finished they were all over each other. No one knew them so to all intense and purposes they were just like any other young couple having a good night out!

Much much later when he could hear the heavy breathing of Mrs Jones sleeping did Mack allow himself to think about what he had done! He knew that Nichola Jones was fond of him; but they certainly weren't boyfriend/girlfriend material; no disrespect but an estranged husband and a child was too much baggage for Mack; he was too much of a child himself never mind having to complete with a toddler for its mothers attention! Even if the sex was something else; his body was yet again sore off her biting and scratching and he hoped against hope that Craig or anyone else hadn't been wandering the corridors of the hotel and heard Mrs Jones screaming and shouting!

But the deed was done; again. All thoughts of arriving in 'coupledom' with Melissa had been shot into oblivion; why was he even kidding himself he could settle down with one woman when he so easily could jump into bed with the first bit of temptation set in his path! He was suddenly very sober!

Back in his own hotel room he tried to recap what Madame Zeta Marie had said; he could remember nothing apart from her cold porcelain like doll like face! Just as the sleep came, he remembered; she had asked him for a question; the only thing that had been running through his head at the time was his go to song when confronted with a pretty face; 'Oh

Na Na What's my Name!' Not Gran like Madame Zeta Marie had said; it was Nan; his Nan; and Madame Zeta Marie had been calling his name, hadn't she? She had been calling 'Mack? Mack? As he bolted out of her little booth! How could she have known it??? His battered and bruised body shivered with goose pimples! Sleep didn't come easy!

(67) This is the Last Time   **#keane**

The final day of training passed uneventful; three days learning about various types of finance was enough for everyone and when the little test came at the end they all just ploughed into it and emerged from the conference room with little certificates basically saying that they were now experts in selling that specific company's finance packages!

Their flight home wasn't going to be until the following morning; there was only one flight to Newcastle each day and even though there was a more regular train service; they would still not arrive back in the North East until the small hours of the following morning; it made more sense just to stay another night!

Mack sensed more trouble. Craig had opted to go to some sort of festival with the older facilitator he had grown fond of under the strict instruction that Craig would have to be returned to the hotel by midnight if he had any chance of making the early morning flight home. That left Mack with Mrs Jones!!!! There had been no mention of their rumble around the bed the night before; it was very much business as usual with lovely Mrs Jones; but Mack really didn't fancy spending a whole night alone in his hotel room; his mind was far too much in overdrive what with his shenanigans with Mrs Jones and the creepy interlude with Madame Zeta Marie!

He couldn't just leave her to her own devices; he didn't want to; he didn't want to be alone. Mrs Jones suggested going to see a film; he jumped at the chance. It was a bizarre night; as a couple they were intimate; they were work colleagues and hoped that they could be friends. They sat in the cinema watching some romcom of Mrs Jones's choosing; sharing a bucket of pop corn and the warmth of feeling another person's leg pressing against you in the darkness! Film over they made their way into a little restaurant serving pizza and spent the next couple of hours getting to know each other; no holds barred!

Mrs Jones really was lovely. She had flirted outrageously with Mack from the moment she set eyes on him; they had shared some frantic sex; but sitting in front of him; she was just a really nice young woman; a different place and a different time and maybe they could have had something. It would never happen; they both knew that; but somewhere between the potato skins and the Bailey's coffee they created a bond. Mack had a feeling they were going to be friends for a long long time!

She was easy to talk to. He told her about Carly; how he had continuingly cheated on her; how he had came a cropper when he got involved with Jude Johnson; Mrs Jones did say if he ever did come across a copy of the video she would love to see it; the saucy minx. And in return Mrs Jones told him how much she was missing her husband and the life they should have together. Madam Zeta Marie had told her she needed to build bridges; Mrs Jones agreed. She said being a single parent wasn't the life for her; she should be helping her husband find a job not ridiculing him for it; they would have more chance of a better life together than apart.

Mrs Jones even apologised for leading Mack up the proverbial garden path; he assured her she hadn't; he just hoped that they could be friends; even if she reconciled with Mr Jones! They would be; she said she would always be grateful for what happened between them; he had given her confidence!

Meal over; there was nothing else to do but leave restaurant and return to the hotel. Both unsure what would happen next; 'coffee in her room?' she said. Why not. This time when they ended up back in her bed it was less frantic. They both knew it would be the last time so took their time; she kissed all his scratches and bruises and in return he kissed her in her sweetest spot until she screamed; but this time the screams were muffled in a pillow; none of the howling of their previous encounters. And then he left. As he climbed into his own bed, he even felt a pang of sadness; there would be no more me and Mrs Jones; not intimately anyway; but he also felt like a prize shit. Not once in the whole evening he had spent with Mrs Jones did he give the lovely Melissa a thought!!

(68) The Boys are Back in Town   #thinlizzy

Mack met Marty in the pub they could only describe as their local. When they were young and drinking in pubs was all new to them; The Swan had been their second home. They would meet up in the back room which homed a pool table and all the boys would hang out there either until closing time; or they went off into town or something. Back in the day they could be there every Friday Saturday and Sunday; especially if there was football on; there would always be someone there Mack could have a pint and a game of pool with.

Nowadays they went to The Swan seldomly. Sometimes at Christmas they would try and have a meet up there with all the old boys; but each year there was fewer and fewer of them and whereas they would always make for the back room; now there were a new generation of boys making a commotion and playing at being Billy Big Balls in the room they had once called theirs!

So Mack and Marty sat in the bar; relegated to where all the old timers sat. He was getting old! The Swan itself hadn't changed a bit. Even down to the bar staff; they were older but they all still recognised the two friends when they stood at the bar waiting to be served their pints. For Mack it had a nice familiar comfort blanket feel to it! Just what he needed after his few days away!

Nursing their pints Mack and Marty caught up with what had been going on in their lives since the last time. Reggie was doing well; Dina was getting big and Marty had taken on even more responsibility at work! Mack filled Marty in on everything at Len Pearson Cars and all the bits inbetween; Melissa; Mrs Jones; Elle; Jenny! It was ridiculous because all that had happened within five or six weeks; he even told Marty about Madam Zeta Marie!!

Marty had laughed; he said nowadays he couldn't compete; he had well and truly had his wings clipped! But Mack could see he was happy; all the sorrow of the year before seemed to be melting away from him and was now replaced by a proud daddy who had unexpectedly had the centre of his world moved. Mack couldn't imagine ever having that type of contentment. He had come close with Carly; but that was only on the surface; if he hadn't been caught out he would no doubt have been behaving badly behind her back still and getting away with it!

He liked that he could just be himself with Marty; he knew everything there was to know about Mack; well almost. There had always been one small snippet of information he hadn't share with his best friend; Mini! He hoped he would never have to. But apart from Mini there was nothing he hadn't shared with him! Oh and Christina; he had failed to mention Christina! But apart from those two episodes in Mack's life; Marty knew everything!

As if Marty could read his mind; the next topic of conversation was the postponed Christening of Reggie; Mack had been asked to be his Godfather; a role he had accepted with relish; but the half made booking had been delayed when Dina had found out she was pregnant again. The plan was that once the new baby had made its arrival; both the children would be baptised together. According to what Marty was saying it would be sometime in the Spring; and woe and betide Mack if he couldn't get the Sunday off!

But the thing that Mack had thought his friend had tapped in to was Mini; Marty's younger sister. She wasn't actually called Mini; she was Milly; but over the years her nick name had stuck and Mini was the name she was known as. Milly Cooper; became Mini Cooper!

Anyway the mention of Mini was due to the fact that she was Reggie's other Godparent along with Dina's cousin whose name escaped them both. But Mini had taken herself off to some Greek Island in the Summer and had so far failed to return home! Marty wasn't worried; Mini had always been strong and independent; he just hoped that she would be back in time to perform her Godparent duties!

Mack had always liked Marty's little sister; she was only a year or two younger than the boys and like her brother had confidence by the bucket load. And that was how Mini Cooper became Mack's guilty secret. According to the teenage version of Mini; she had been crushing on Mack since he was five; which Mack believed to be true because whenever he was at Marty's house; Mini would be there too. Marty thought she was a pest and would yell at his mam and dad to have her removed from wherever they were; Mack thought she was cute and always made time for her.

When they were older the three of them would hang out for hours together playing on computer games; Mini was as adapt on the Playstation as the other two; Mack still didn't mind her being there; Marty hated it and in turn started to hate her; which cause no end of arguments in the Cooper household!

(69) Young Girl   #garypucket&theuniongap

By the time Marty and Mack left school; Mini was a big Mack fan. He didn't mind; he was used to having lots of female attention by then; and Mini was like the little sister he never had. He never minded her texting him and he always made time for her if he saw her; he didn't lead her on; he was her brother's mate and there was an unspoken rule about your mates sister; you just didn't do it!

But then of course Mack did. Mini was probably about 18 by then; the weird thing for Mack was that she was the spit and dab of her brother; if Marty wore a wig and shoved a couple of tennis balls down his top then it would be 'voila Mini'!
So, sleeping with Mini had been a sort of surreal experience; only ever happening once and never to be repeated.

And good to both of their word; they hadn't!

It was like sleeping with Mack had cured Mini's itch and she never looked at Mack in the same way again.

Or had he been a disappointment?? To be fair he had been quite drunk; it had been someone or others 21st and Mini had been there; he said he would make sure she got home safely and he had. He had also followed her into the dark house and up the stairs past his friend's familiar bedroom and into her less familiar one. It was bizarre; in his drunken haze he could see Marty's face!

It obviously wasn't Marty; but her features were so similar.

If he had underperformed then that would be the reason why.

Mini didn't seem to want him to stay; he certainly didn't want to emerge from her bedroom the following morning; so he made his way past the familiar bedroom door of his friend and out of the house!

From the outside Mack and Mini's relationship would appear not to have changed. But to them it had; they had tasted the forbidden fruit; and like all things that you wait and wait and wait for; it hadn't tasted half as good as they had hoped for!

But it had happened; and it would be one experience he would take to his grave with him! That and Christina; who had been Marty and Mini's babysitter! Another episode he would never divulge to his best friend! Another certain someone he should never have been with!

Seeing Mini at Reggie and the new baby's christening wouldn't be a problem; what happened between Mack and Mini had happened years ago and they had always kept in touch since then; to all intense and purposes nothing had changed. When Marty had been at his lowest after his friend's death; it had been Mini and Mack that made sure that he was always safe; that there was always someone available to check and make sure he was all right. So there was no problem about them celebrating Reggie's and the new baby's special day!

Marty was ready to make tracks home; he didn't like staying out too late with Dina being pregnant and Reggie teething so after another quick pint for the road; they went their separate ways!

(70) Hometown Glory   #adele

Mack was unsure what to do. It was Friday night! His mam and Tom's date night and it was barely 9 o'clock; he never went home on a Friday before 11. He thought of texting Melissa; she had been in touch all the time he had been away, and she had already text to say that she was out on the Friday Night Ritual with the Call Centre lot and was in a pub in town!

Tempting as it was Mack thought better of it. He did genuinely want to see Melissa; he had missed her; well, he had missed her in the short spaces of time he had been on his own; beyond that, when he was crawling all over Mrs Jones; he hadn't given her a second thought. But he would have liked to gone and had a catch up with her; tell her about his little jaunt South and see what she had been up to in his absence; he would lay his life on it that no one would have been crawling up and down her body!

But there was no way he could go. The bruises and scratches all over his body were testament to a night spent with someone else. Melissa didn't deserve to be hurt like that; she was nice; she deserved better. He had told her he wanted an early night because he was working all weekend and she seemed happy to believe that. He was going to try his best to distance himself from her; again! Any thought that he had a chance of riding off with her into the sunset at the beginning of the week had surely been well and truly scuppered by the end.

Deciding that he would walk home via the local chippy shop for a fish and chip supper; he once again threw Melissa to the Gods! He would keep his head down at work; God knows he needed the money, and it would be an excuse to put Melissa well and truly on a back burner; avoiding hurting her feelings and becoming a bigger tosser than he already was!

And he needed to get back to the gym. He hadn't been at all since he started working at Len Pearson Cars. His usual quite healthy diet had gone out of the window and he lost count of the takeaways and meals out he had eaten recently. The chippy tea would be his last supper. Healthy eating: healthy mind and weekly trips to the gym were on the cards. And this all gave him a spring in his step as he wandered the streets home. It wasn't a bad night, and the walk was clearing his head. It had been quite a week!

As with Mack though the night didn't quite end up the way he had intended. It was way way after 11 by the time he got home; the house was quiet as a mouse. His mam and Tom must have been settled for hours. Getting into bed and putting his alarm on for work he was surprised to see that he would only be getting about 3 hours sleep! And he was starving! He never got his fish and chip supper!

You see just as he was turning the corner into the street where the chippy was, he ran flat bang into Emma. Well, that wasn't strictly true; she was driving her car and he was waiting at the kerb until the flash BMW passed. It didn't. It slowed right down and pulled up next to the kerb where he was standing. A moment of unease passed through Mack; was he about to be mugged or something; the night was still young but it was dark as was the nights in October; maybe the driver thought he was drunk and an easy target. Mack took his hands out of his pockets; if not to punch someone to at least give himself a bit of momentum if he needed to run away!

The window came down and a voice said 'whats a good looking boy like you wandering the streets at this time of night?' He knew the voice instantly and she must have flicked the interior light on because suddenly he could see Emma Tiding as clear as day! Relief coursed through his body; he wasn't going to be attacked or mugged or kidnapped; or worse whatever that could be!

Emma Tiding! Mack hadn't seen her for a few years; she had been one of his girls when he left school. She was the one he would often stumble home with at the end of a night out if he hadn't found anywhere else to be! She used to say she was just his backup plan; but sometimes if he knew they were in town at the same time; he would text her knowing that whatever taxi rank he said he would be going to she would be there. She was less of a backup plan and more of a sure thing.

Relationship wise they had never really got it together; they were friends as Mack always tried to be with girls he slept with; he didn't do bad terms well; Carly was testament to that; as much as he had shit on and hurt her; he still wanted her to like him deep down; he wanted to be one of the good bad guys. So far it hadn't worked out that way with Carly.

Emma was a different fish. They had just drifted apart over the years and the times he met her in the taxi rank grew to be few and far between. Facebook notified him that she was in a relationship and not being one to step on another blokes toes if he could help it; he left well alone and they didn't really see each other again.

(71) Somebody That I Used to Know   #gotye

But there she was in some swanky BMW which wouldn't look out of place being driven by some local hoodlum or drug dealer; something he knew neither Emma or her bloke were. Emma was a primary school teaching assistant and if his memory served him rightly; her bloke worked on the roads.

She was looking good and obviously pleased to see him. They spent a few minutes chit chatting before she asked if he fancied a quick drink. Even if he went and got his supper; he knew he would still too early to go home and break the unspoken rule about disturbing his mam and Tom's alone time. So he found himself in the passenger seat of Emma's BMW and heading out of town.

As it always been with Emma; there were no awkward silences; they talked about her job; he had been right she was a teaching assistant and they talked about his new job and significantly the BMW they were riding about in. It wasn't Emma's! Her own car was a Corsa which she said had seen better days; she even hinted that she may come to his garage and see what her options would be with regard to part exchanging it! Tick thought Mack; that would be his sale and made a mental note to make sure he had her current mobile number!

And then they were sitting in a pub on the outskirts of town. It was chocker block; it was a Friday so it went without saying that the world and his wife were in there. But there were a couple of tables available and after getting drinks at the bar; Mack found himself sitting opposite the very familiar Emma Tiding.

Time had been good to Emma. The amount of times Mack had bumped into old school friends; sometimes with the embarrassment that you got when you didn't actually recognise them; age hadn't suited them. A once pretty little 16 year old sometimes was a million miles away from the 5 year older version of themselves. But not so Emma Tiding.

If anything, she looked a lot better than Mack could ever remember her being. Younger she always had an edge about her. She had been a bit of a Chav. Too much make-up; too much hair; too few clothes. She had been Mack's sure thing for a long time; but on reflection he thought that was maybe because her younger days look had put a lot of blokes off. But maybe he was being harsh. Maybe she didn't look that much different to all of the girls of that time. Maybe she was his sure thing because she had wanted to be.

The had never talked about them being on more of a permanent footing. It had been good drunken sex; lots of good drunken sex. But in the morning; after her mam had made them both breakfast; he would leave their house without a backward glance. Until next time! Had she wanted more???

Mack squirmed on his seat a bit. On reflection maybe he had been a shit to her. Fuck! But it couldn't have been that bad; or if it had been she must have forgiven him or else why would she be sitting in a pub with him now looking all voluptuous!

Here we go Mack thought to himself and in his head that old automatic mantra clicked on to play 'oh na na…..'

(72) Hey Mama   #beberexha

Emma was chatting; and with the mantra theme tune playing in his head. Mack took the opportunity to have a good look at Emma. She was certainly looking good. Everything about her was softer looking. She was still blonde; but more highlights and less brass; and her make-up was now subtle. Time had suited her well.

She was telling him about her job; she worked with someone they went to school with but for the life of him Mack had no recollection who the bloke was; if he had played football with him like Emma was suggesting; he must have been shite because he had made no impact.

Feigning recollection. Mack looked Emma up and down. Her boobs!! In his eyes he had only done a fly past with his eyes; but he had taken then in. The Emma of old was all push up bra and chicken fillets; they had often launched the aforementioned chicken fillets at the end of a drunken night when they were unwrapping each other. She had always had tiny boobs; or in Emma's words 'a handful because anything more than that was a waste'. But the ones he had skim read looked real; and there was so much more than a handful there!

Trying not to focus on them and concentrate on her face; she had now given up on Mack ever remembering the PE teacher at her school and was telling him her latest news. She was going to have a baby!!!

Check Mack thought; definitely nothing to do with him. But he hadn't noticed her pregnancy in the car; or when they walked into the pub together or even sitting there. But he was thrilled for her. Standing up; she pulled her top tight to her and there it was; a huge bump – well a six month bump!! Looking at her she was absolutely glowing, and Mack was thrilled for her. She would make a lovely mam.

Somewhere in the back of his mind he could remember Emma looking after her little brothers and sisters; and if he remembered rightly there had been quite a few of them in different shapes and sizes when he wolfed down his 'hangover' breakfast at her house. Emma would always have time for them no matter how hungover she was. Yes she would be a natural.

He bought them another drink. Now the orange juice made sense; not just because she was driving.

Anyway she said; she was glad she had seen him. It had been nice having a catch up, but she also had something she wanted to tell him. She wasn;'t sure if it was common knowledge yet; but thought it would be better coming from her than anyone else, or finding out on Instagram or Facebook.

He was all ears!!!

The long and the short of it was that she had been to the Health Centre a couple of weeks earlier; one of her ante-natal appointments. No easy way to say it she said so she just said it. Carly was pregnant!!!

Mack felt like he had been slapped across the face.

He hadn't been expecting that. It had been a bit of a shock him not noticing Emma's pregnancy but now his ex-girlfriend seemed to be in the same condition. He didn't need to do a check with her either; no way it would ever be his baby.

Carly having a baby?? When they had been together there had never been talk of any babies; the plans they made were seeing the world; just the two of them. There had been no near misses with them; Carly used to go for some injection thing and their baby worries were over for the next year or so. A baby for Carly seemed to be something that would need to be planned for!

Mack had forgot Emma and Carly had known each other. Small town though and although Carly had gone to a different school from them; she had been friends with lots who did go to theirs and of course Emma and Carly's would have crossed. Even through Mack but if they had met before when he was with Carly; he wouldn't have said anything. He had a girl in every port so to speak, but as was his way, he always kept stum about them.

They had met at the Health Centre again, Carly had congratulated Emma on her pregnancy, they had been trying for some time by all accounts. And then Carly had told her the good news about her baby; first appointment so early days. But still. Emma seeing Mack that night seemed to be a sign; it had been the decent thing to do seeing as Mack and Carly had so much history.

It was a sucker punch.

(73) Man in the Mirror   #michaeljackson

Emma offered to drive Mack home. He turned it down, it was getting late and Emma should really be home and tucked up in her bed. But Mack the car salesman made sure that he had her mobile before waving her off and watching the lights of the swanky BMW head off into the distance.

Mack walked home. No Mack stomped home in a zig zag fashion. He got to the end of his street and kept on going. He needed to burn off some of the energy that had built up inside him since Emma had told him the news!

He had been hungry, but a couple of more pints in and the hunger was surpressed; the smell of the chippy when he walked past churned his stomach. He had no right to be feeling as churned up as he was; but still. He couldn't help it. She had been his girl. Obviously not his only girl or he would have been the daddy.

So he kept walking. Around and around. Not far from home; a run would probably have been better for him, but the drink would have made him puke, so walking it was. The streets became quiet; the lights in the houses went off and the only cars that passed him were taxis. And eventually his mind started to still.

Carly would always be his Achilles heel. The relationship that had got away. The relationship that there was literally no way back to, not even as friends. But he hadn't really learned anything had he? He still had Melissa in his life and she had hopes of coupledom; so did he! In his head anyway. She was nice. Just like Carly was nice. Neither of them had done anything wrong. Maybe him and Carly jumped into the happy family thing a bit too early; they had been friends for so long and then when they did get together they just wanted to be with each other all of the time, so a flat seemed the perfect solution.

But it had quickly became routine; like life does. But instead of adjusting himself; Mack had wanted it all; the thrill of the chase when reality there was nothing to chase Carly for; he had it all. He was stupid and seeking thrills beyond the little flat they shared had been his downfall.

And now he was doing it all over again. Melissa kept him interested, but only when she was standing right in front of him. When she was out of his eyeshot, he was off. How many times since he met her? 3 or 4; he couldn't remember.

Melissa was nice. Too nice for Mack and his shenanigans. Bites and bruises aside; he shouldn't and wouldn't see her this weekend. He was throwing her back to the Gods.

It was late; he had work in the morning. He seemed to have shaken off the shock of Carly's pregnancy and the mood. Nothing else to do but head home. Tomorrow was a new day!

(74) Foundations #katenash

Mack really was starting to get the hang of his job.

He still had to ask a million questions; not so much the paperwork side of things, he had his very good friend Mrs Jones to help with that. She wouldn't let him fall. They seemed to have developed a special bond that only people who know each other intimately can have, even if they were no longer intimate. They had each other's backs, well Mrs Jones had Mack's, he had no reason to be watching out for her, she was in control.

The cars were a whole different ball game for Mack though. His knowledge of cars was as good as the next mans, any man that didn't sell them for a living. There were just so many variations and even though every scrap of information there was about each car at his fingertips, he struggled.

John was truly an Oracle, but Kevin wasn't far behind him. Mack never see them running backwards and forward to their desk to check on specs when they were dealing a customer. Nor Justin that much for that matter. But for Mack he was always running a marathon, from the pitch to his desk, back to the pitch, then again to his desk. It went on and on.

But then John let him into a little secret, the majority of the times, they just winged it!

If they thought they had mis-informed someone, they would check the facts and call them later. That simple. Mack could have kissed him. He was beginning to think he was just thick.

It worked. If he could say something that resembled the right answer, the customer was happy and would sign up on the car. With this gem of information, Mack found he began to sell more cars. It was really all just about confidence. If he sounded like he knew what he was doing and not have to fact check everything, then people had confidence in him.

Mack was loving his life. His total concentration remained on his job. Mrs Jones was ticked off and boxed away. Carly's baby news was now digested, regretted and boxed away, for now anyway. Elle Pearson – pending. Melissa – ongoing but in a box without a lid for when his bruised body would allow it.

He went back to the gym most days, it made him feel better and when he was looking after his body, he watched what he ate. Melissa seemed to be happy having regular texts chats, he explained he was just busy with work and wanted to start making proper money for his bonus, then they could do better things. Mack hadn't quite thrown back Melissa to the God's, more kept her dangling with carrots! He liked her, she was good go be with, but until he was sure that he could keep his John Thomas firmly tucked inside his pants, he couldn't keep dragging her down the garden path.

And he was managing. Work and gym seemed to be keeping him out of mischief. He was even thinking of booking him and Melissa a table at a new restaurant that had opened in town and where half of Len Pearson Cars were raving about, but then his mam had reminded him he was going to watch Newcastle United play the following Saturday with Becky. He had forgot all about it. It was a tea time kick off so it wasn't a problem with work, but he didn't want to go to game and then have to rush off to meet Melissa. If Becky had access all areas then he didn't want to miss out.

(75) Greatest Day   #takethat

He loved Newcastle United, he had done the stadium tours when he was a young lad and had been to countless games. But he had never been with anyone that had anything to do with the club. Becky being a physio must have known quite a few of the players. No the restaurant could wait, as could Melissa, he might even suggest going out on the Sunday afternoon, that would be a nice thing to do.

Paula had given Mack quite a little lecture before he left for the match. He had literally only spent 15 minutes in the house changing out of his work stuff and into his Newcastle shirt and jeans and all the time Paula had chuntered on about how he hadn't got to take advantage of Becky and her position at the club. He argued back saying that Becky was a grown woman and if she found him attractive that wasn't his fault. It was all said with a grin on his face, he had no intention of taking advantage of Becky, just her clout at the club. Not that he told his mam that!!

And what a night he had. It didn't even bother him that he watched the match on his own, this was Newcastle United and anyone who you sat next to was your new best buddy.

Mack hadn't thought that he wouldn't be with Becky watching the game, but of course she was working and her seat was down beside he dugout. But she had left him a ticket at the box office, where as instructed he went to when he arrived at the ground.

At first he was a little nervous, he had never been to a game on his own. But he had a mint seat near the directors box and he could see the BBC Sport commentary team in the corner. And if he strained his head he thought that he could see Alan Shearer – woop woop, Gary Linekar and was that Ashley Cole?? He couldn't be sure.

He was early for the game, he watched the teams warming up. Newcastle United were playing West Ham, a favourite team of his so he was no hardship sitting in the almost empty ground. He could see someone waving from the touchline, Becky! He barely recognised her in her workwear, which was the same as everyone else associated with Newcastle United currently on the pitch. He waved back and then as if by magic, the floodgates opened and the ground was a burning cauldron of noise.

It was one of the best nights of Mack's life!!

Newcastle United won, Becky was waiting for him as he dismounted the stairs after the game, she took him into the back rooms where the players cooled off and got patched up if their injuries weren't too serious. He was completely star struck, no words just nods of the head as the players wandered around from room to room!

Mack sat and took it all in and when Becky said she wouldn't be long and went to get changed, he had the urge to get his phone out and start taking photographs of the now empty corridor, but still. This was St James Park and behind each of the closed doors was an absolute super star, it was what every Geordie lad's dreams were made of. But he didn't, mainly because he didn't want to get Becky into trouble, she was his now new best friend. Marty who?? He smirked to himself thinking what his best friend would think of him sitting in the changing rooms, well corridor which led to the changing rooms at Newcastle United.

Becky was back. Did he fancy a drink?? Did he not. Thinking that they would be going to one of the bars inside the ground, he was surprised when she asked him if he had a car with him.. He did, it was parked up beside Leazes Park, nearest he could get to the ground. They were apparently going in his car then, hers was parked in the ground and would be safe enough there if she decided that she would have a few drinks.

They walked and they talked. To Mack she was one of the most interesting women he had ever met. She told him how she had got into football, that she had been to PSG as a trainee; Paris Saint Germain: there had been a job opportunity but the Newcastle United one had materialised at the same time and it was a no brainer. When she qualified, she made her way home to Newcastle.

Becky seemed to be impressed with the truck, said that she had looked at one for herself, but it hadn't been practical for all the city centre driving she did, so had plumbed for a more sedate Kia.

They headed out of town, Mack had no idea where they were going, but was so high on life that he just did as he was told as she told him to turn right or left or straight across at the roundabout. Before he knew it they were pulling up outside an Italian Restaurant that looked way beyond anything Mack could have afforded. Becky must have seen the shock on his face, but assured him that it was one of the perks of the job. After a game, all the backroom staff would head off for food and drink, sometimes to drown their sorrows, but on a night like tonight with a win under their belts, they would all be there, slapping themselves and each other on the back about what a grand job with the team.

Mack knew no one bar Becky. But he knew who they were talking about and soaked up the atmosphere, the beer and the delicious food that kept arriving out of the kitchen. Everyone was friendly and before long, Mack was at ease and even managed to ask a few questions about players he was really interested in.

Meal over, they continued to sit around the table. He leaned into Becky and told her how thankful he was that she had invited him to the match and hoped that she would invite him again.

For the first time that day, he looked at Becky! She had short hair and in the soft light of the restaurant, she looked like a little pixie. When she had waved at him at the ground, he had thought it was a boy waving. But now sitting next to him, her features were soft and very feminine. As if she knew what he was thinking she told him to look around the table.

Men, they were all men there. Apart from the odd girlfriend or wife, the ones that worked for the club were all men.

Becky laughed. She ran her fingers through her hair, something stirred within Mack. He had drank too much, he wasn't wearing beer goggles, Becky was pretty. But his inhibitions were always diluted the more he drank. He had promised Paula faithfully that he wouldn't make a move on Becky.

'It's a man's world, it's survival. It's easier!' Becky said. She had never said, but in tracksuits with her short hair, they thought that she was a lesbian and tended to leave her alone. It was the easiest way. Pulling out her phone, Becky started showing Mack pictures of her on nights out. Her hair was long, sometimes blonde, sometimes brunette, or red or pink. All thanks to a variety of wigs she kept for special occasions!

With her stock of long hair, she was more a Goddess than a pixie. Deep breaths, Mack thought to himself. Don't be going there. But the gentleman that he was, which in truth was Paula's fault because she had always told him to tell a lady she looked lovely. He found that his mouth was open and he was telling Becky what a looker she was with or without the wigs.

Laughing she told him he was sworn to secrecy, the blokes around the table would have her life if they knew that beneath the tracksuits and trainers, she was actually quite a girly girl who could do a mean Macarena in a pair of heels.

(76) Hands to Myself   #selenagomez

They ended up sitting in the restaurant until last orders. More drinks, less inhibitions. Mack had drank far too much to drive himself home, so was happy to jump in a taxi with Becky and get dropped off when she had been safely deposited at her door.

That was the plan anyway. But half an hour later he found himself in her living room having yet another drink. Mack really wasn't sure how it had happened, he did seem to think that the taxi didn't have time to make the 30 minute journey to his house from Becky's but in the fuzz of his drunken mind, Mack did seem to think that there would be another taxi collecting him in an hour or so.

Becky was sweet. She was obviously doing well for herself. Her home was a new build and considering she lived there alone, it was quite big. They got along really well, there were no awkward gaps and although they were both tiddly, Mack found her really interesting. Nothing to do with the amount of his sporting heroes that she had met. Her mobile was full of pictures with not just footballers, but manager and pundits. And other famous people from other sports. He couldn't believe that she had met them all. He had bumped in to Chris Waddle in Asda once and another time he had seen Peter Beardsley when he had been in Tesco Extra at about 3 in the morning doing a munchie shop with Carly once, well he thought it was, he was wearing a hat so couldn't be sure.

Mack thought Becky was awesome!

As much as he was trying not to go onto Mack Attack mode, it was difficult not to when he was a little bit worse for wear and they were sitting so close to each other looking at her mobile.

When the taxi that they thought they had booked didn't materialise, Mack knew he was in trouble. The old mantra started playing in his head. 'Oh na na na ……' But it was less his Nan and more his mam he was thinking about. She would bloody kill him.

But there was no choice. It was late and he knew that they would struggle to get a taxi at that time of night. Becky offered him a bed for the night, he refused and said he would make do with the settee if that was okay with her. He really didn't want to be climbing the stairs up to a bedroom, he knew what direction that would take. A wonky one.

Happy that he was staying, Becky got them another drink and for the time it took for them to finish it off, they talked about their lives!! For only really just meeting that day, they were very comfortable in each other's company. They especially talked about their mam's, if there was one thing that was going to dampen down Mack's ever growing want for the elf like Becky, it was going to be talking about his mam to his potential step sister.

Like Mack, Becky and her little sister Lucy had been brought up by their mam. Tom had left when they were little, not because either her mam or dad had done anything wrong, they were just making each other unhappy and decided that rather than bring the girls up in a miserable home, they would go their separate ways and be the best parents they could be.

It had worked. They had spent most weekends with their dad and whenever there had been anything going on, birthday parties, Christmas etc, they had always put on a united front and done it as a family.

Becky's mam was married to someone else now, but she hadn't done that until the girls were old enough to understand. Tom it appeared had a succession of bad relationships, some of which Becky regaled Mack with. But both Lucy and Becky had agreed that he had hit the jackpot when he had met Paula. They hoped that she was the one.

Mack agreed, his mam was amazing and he also agreed that Tom was a decent bloke. Trying to dampen the static that seemed to be fizzing between them, he even said that one day they might be brother and sister.

It seemed to do the trick. There were no more drinks being offered. Just a duvet and a pillow.

Lying in the dark living room, Mack wasn't sure if he was pleased or not. Becky truly was awesome, it wasn't just the job, there was something about her. She oozed femininity which was surprising as she spent all her days in a man's world pretending that she wasn't interested in men at all. But that was maybe why, when she wasn't around her workfolk and she let her hair down. Or in Becky's case put her hair on, she oozed sex appeal.

Never the less, Mack was pleased with himself. He could put his hand on his heart and say to Paula that there had been no hanky-panky, that they had both been on their best behaviour, but Becky was his new best friend. Marty who????

(77) Enjoy Yourself   #thespecials

Mack slept in one of those funny sleeps you have when you drink too much, but not enough to comatose you. A stupor did they call it. He slept fitfully in parts, it wasn't the settee, it was a huge four seater thing so there was plenty of room for him and he had slept in worse places. He just seemed to be unsettled.

But sleep eventually came and he was off in the land of nod. For a while anyway. His dreams were tormenting, women, lots of women. Carly, Melissa, Elle, Stacey's mom, all parading in technicolour before his very eyes. Scantily clad and teasing. Oh and Becky, she put in an appearance there too. And a few girls he hadn't thought about for year. They were graphic images. Even in his sleep he could feel himself stirring in his boxers. It all felt so real to him. One of them was using her mouth on him. Fuck it felt real. What a dream.

It was real!!

Mack's eyes were open and he was awake, but there was still someone there giving him pleasure. Not someone. Becky!!

He didn't dare move. All he could do was lie back and think of England. He was desperate to put his hand down and touch her pixie cut hair, but he didn't, he just lay back and let her work her magic on him. That mouth, those hands. If he touched her he would end up doing the deed and that would be wrong. He had been so proud of himself toning down the Mack Attack and not succumbing to temptation and a pretty face.

Becky was good. She definitely wasn't the lesbian. He was putty in her hands. Well not putty or in her hands, her mouth and one of her little hands. She did something with her tongue and he was gone. Within minutes so was she. If his winky wasn't still out of his boxer shorts he wouldn't have believed it had happened.

This time he slept dreamlessly. When her heard Becky shouting his name it was daylight and she was standing next to him with a cup of coffee. She didn't look like she had been on a night time adventure into his boxer shorts, she looked exactly like she had done at the match the day before. But even nursing a hangover he knew it had happened.

Embarrassed that he was only wearing a t-shirt and his boxer shorts, he waited until she had left the room, then scrambled into his jeans and rest of his clothes.

By the time he had finished his coffee, Becky was dressed for the day and ready to drop him off for his truck in her taxi. The conversation was as it should be as the drove along. So much so that Mack did begin to wonder if it had just been part of his dream. But he knew different. It had once been a wakeup call off Carly, he used to lie there and pretend he was asleep, until he could feign it no more. Nope, Becky had been on a little adventure in his boxer shorts. He just didn't know if he should say anything about it.

As it was, he never got opportunity. Becky's phone rang and she spent the remainder of the journey talking to her colleague about her workload later that day. Which of the players would be coming in to see her, what injuries he thought they had picked up. Mack was buzzing, not that players had injuries, but that they were talking about the Newcastle United superstars in such a blaze manner.

Becky was still on her call as the taxi pulled up behind his truck. There was nothing else he could do but wave a bye to her and mouth a 'text me' before she was off and he was left holding his truck keys and wondering what the past 24 hours had been all about.

Wow!!!

Beside's the football which had been awesome, he had never had anyone do that to him through the night that he one had never even kissed or two wanted anything back in return, it always ended in repaying the favour. Becky had simply done the deed and left. 'What the fuck!'

Who would have thought it. Little Becky! But if she was trying to attract his attention, it had worked and she had it!

Back home his mam was in the kitchen. She gave him one of those looks that said 'well' without having to utter a word. 'I stayed at Becky's but I didn't touch her!! Granddad's life!!' He replied in the childish jargon he always used when trying to prove a point. Technically he was telling the truth. He hadn't touched her, she had touched him. He didn't instigate anything. If anything she had violated him. But this snippet of information he would just keep to himself and certainly not tell Paula who was still looking at him as if he had really been up to something!

It was Sunday so that meant only one thing Sunday lunch. He had only had warmed up ones over the past few weeks. He had worked Sunday's but now that he was much more proficient at his job, he was on the rota properly and every third Sunday would be a day of rest. It would be nice to sit at the dining room table with his mam and Granddad.

He had no other plans. He had thought of going and having a few pints with some of his mates, chances were there would be one or two of them out, but after the drinks off the previous day, he wasn't really feeling it. A day in the house watching crap films seemed like a very good idea. He was hoping for a busy week.

So while Mack waited for Sunday dinner, he had a soak in the bath and a little reminisce about what had happened in his boxer short area the night before, he had then lain on his bed, switched on his telly and thought about Newcastle United and Becky.

He really did think she was awesome. And really quite pretty, in the pictures of her in those wigs she had been drop dead gorgeous. Obviously clever and very well connected, what wasn't there to like about her. And what she had done to him in the wee hours was a complete head fuck, she had certainly got his attention. And more!!

Mack was surprised that Tom was there for lunch. He didn't go every weekend but much to Mack's surprise they were off for a few days away, but because Sunday Lunch was the highlight of her dad's week, they had decided that they wouldn't go until Sunday evening. So there was Tom, already sitting at the table talking to his Granddad about Newcastle United's performance the day before.

In the end Mack spent lunch talking about the match and Becky and her work mates and what footballers he had seen and all the time there was the thought of Becky on her knees in the middle of the night with her little mouth giving him a completely different type of physio!!

(78) Rose Garden   #lynnanderson

Mack never liked being in the house on his own. It was something that didn't happen often. At teatime his Granddad had jumped in his car and made his way back to his own house and his Mam had jumped in Tom's car and sped off into the night and to some hotel they had booked for the start of their little trip.

It always felt strange having the whole house to rattle around alone. It never seemed so empty when his mam was just out, but when he knew that she wouldn't be back for a few days he all at once felt a little bit lonely.

Melissa had been texting. Just general chit chat, she hadn't asked to see him and because she hadn't asked to see him, he felt contrary and thought about asking her over. Melissa would certainly help him fill the empty house up. But the thought of Becky was still fresh on his mind and it was, it would be a twats trick to have Melissa over because he wouldn't be able to keep his hands off her.

He felt a bit morose, which wasn't like him. He thought of going for a run, but it was dark outside and raining and he was still weighed down with his roast beef and the crumble and custard he had eaten aswell. But he couldn't sit, he wasn't in the mood for sitting because he would analysis himself and he didn't want to do that. He needed to be on his game for work. If John was right, then the usual trend was that the garage would have another 2 or 3 good weeks and then it would quieten down until January. He needed to make hay when the sun was shining.

Nothing else for it, he had to go for it, he got himself changed, threw on his earphones and took himself off into the dark of night. Rain or no rain, he needed to run the mood off and tire himself out.

Mack didn't think that he suffered with any mental health issues, he had what his mam called a 'sunny disposition' he liked to think that he always looked for the best, in situations, in people. But sometimes, especially after he had a good drink, he would go into a funny mood, not dark or anything, but he always thought that it was if he had gone to sleep drunk and while he was asleep, someone had come and placed a mirror in front of him, so he had no option but to take a good long look at himself.

He knew the mood would pass, it wasn't a huge problem, but it made his normal steady step falter, and it would take him a day or two to get his rhythm back. As he grew older, he found that he could speed the process off by doing something physical like going to the gym or having a run. Hence the November night time run, it didn't stop him thinking, if anything it made him think harder. But usually by the time he had finished exercising and had a shower, he would feel the mood lifting.

He pounded the streets, playlist blasting in his ears and the rain soaking him to the skin. There was nothing wrong, nothing major anyway. Just women. It was always women. They made him and they destroyed him. Look at what Jude had done, but she could never had split him and Carly up if he hadn't given her the ammunition to fire. He had been enthralled by her, she was one of those women who had sussed him out quickly and knew had to keep him entertained. Like Elle, because even with the best will in the world, Mack knew that given the opportunity he would be back there, all over her.

Which made him in turn think about Melissa, the one female in his life who was proper girlfriend material. She was too nice to keep as a friend with benefits. He liked spending time with her, she was funny and sweet and very pretty. And even though she was turning into a saucy little minx, she would never be one of the bold ones. A Stacey's Mom, a Jude, an Elle and now it seemed a Becky! Another female to add to the fold!

A dominating woman who knew what she wanted. As he ran another girl popped into his head. Christina! He had forgot about Christina, how could he have. Christina was the girl next door. Not his girl next door, she had been Marty's girl next door and sometimes babysitter.

She was older than Mack, 10, 12, 15 maybe more years older. She was Marty's mam and dad's next-door neighbour. There had been a boyfriend or husband, Mack could distinctly remember that she had been part of couple. But when he had been young he hadn't really taken that much notice. They had been at events at Marty's house, but to be honest, they had been in descript, just the people that lived next door. No way had Mack ever thought that Christina had been the hot woman next door. Not then anyway.

It wasn't until he was older, much older that he had any dealings with her, and what dealings he had had. Marty's dad had suggested that the boys go and earn themselves some extra money by doing her garden. Apparently Christina had asked if he had known anyone that would be willing to tidy the vast garden up, Marty's dad had suggested the boys. They were both at college by then and always skint. It was summer and it didn't seem too hard a job and the money would be handy, they had grown fond of a night out or two out in town. They would often work on a Saturday, take their pay and then not resurface in the garden for another week.

So Mack and Marty, the infamous M&M started what turned out to be the mammoth task of trimming bushes, weeding and cutting lawns. For some ridiculous reason, they had been given a day rate, something that Christina would surely have lived to regret, because what should have taken them a couple of weekends, dragged out for ages.

By then Christina's significant other half was nowhere to be seen. Mack wasn't sure if he had just left, or died or something. He just wasn't there. After they had been working there for about 6 weeks, Marty got himself a new girlfriend, this one he said was a keeper, so Mack found himself working in the garden on his own.

Christina was very generous. Knowing that Mack was on his own, she would bring him out drinks and snacks and when she handed out his pay at the end of the day, she slipped a little extra in knowing that he was now doing the work of two.

Within 2 or 3 weeks, Christina was helping him in the garden and they were chatting away like old friends. It was the middle of summer and Christina tended to wear short shorts and tee shirts. The shorts would ride up and the tee shirts would gape open. Mack was a man and found himself fascinated with Christina. She wasn't particularly pretty, not in the conventional way. But he had been with plenty of girls by then to know what was sexy and Christina was oozing with it.

But he loved doing the garden, well not doing the garden, but he did like having the money. So any thoughts that he had of making a little move were put on a back burner, although from the body language Christina was hot for Mack, he just didn't want to blow it by misreading the signals.

Then one Saturday they were working away in the garden when a storm cloud burst and before they had chance to run for cover, they were both soaked to the skin. As Christina told him to run for the house, Mack knew that this was it. Cliché, he knew. Wet clothes, hot bodies and all of that, but it was going to be now or never.

And boy it was now!!

Christina insisted that he went upstairs and got out of his wet things and into the hot shower she was going to run. Of course he did as he was told. When Christina arrived in the bathroom, he wasn't surprised. But what did surprise him was what happened next.

Expecting her to join him, he was surprised when she put soap on her hands and started to wash him. It was something that had never happened to him before, he had been in showers with girls, but this was something different. This was Christina taking complete control of the situation and all he could do was stay stock still and let her do whatever it was she wanted to do.

She soaped him everywhere. And when he meant everywhere, it was everywhere. There was nowhere the soap and Christina's fingers didn't go. He was so turned on he didn't think he could cope.

Christina rinsed him off and took him to her bed. She was very much in charge of proceedings. He was putty in her hands. She knew what she wanted and she told him exactly what to do. If his hands started to roam, she smacked him. She smacked him a lot. Christina was amazing! Up until that point he had never been so clean and so dirty! She was a total mind fuck.

Mack never told Marty about Christina. Marty never went back to the gardening so for the remainder of the Summer, Mack was totally Christina's play thing. He would work Saturday and Sundays, sometimes he would even stay over on a Saturday night and Christina would cook them supper and then she would do something amazing to him. She was something else. But once the garden was tidied, it was time for his dalliance to end, it was never anything more than that. But Christina had been another of those women that came into his life and got him. She had got him a lot. And then she had gone.

He was never sure what happened to Christina. Not long after the garden was tidied, the house had gone up for sale, subsequently sold and that was the last of Christina. She was one of those people he never really knew anyone to ask about. He had thought of asking Marty where she had gone, but what was the point, Christina had made it very clear that once the garden had been done there would be no more hook ups. She had never given him her number and had never mention seeing him again. She had used him. And oh how Mack loved her for doing that! He never did find out what happened to her bloke. Maybe he was buried in the garden and that was why she wanted it tidied up! Who knew!!

It was funny, Mack had always thought that it had been Stacey's Mom that had given him a penchant for controlled women, but it truth it had been the unassuming Christina. She didn't have the whistles and bells of Stacey's Mom, but she had certainly been a woman who had known what she wanted. Christina!!

Mack's little trip down memory lane somehow made him feel better. There had always been women, maybe there always would be. Maybe he was doomed to be single. Was it doomed?? Did he want the whole family set up like Marty had?? Maybe he did, but not for a while. Melissa would be a front runner for the whole happy family scenario, she would made a lovely mam. Paula would love her, Melissa had something wholesome about her and Mack knew it she would be someone his mam would take to straightaway.

But the 2.4 children thing was a long long way off. Mack couldn't stay faithful to Melissa now, what chance would there be with they were living an everyday life together. Look what had happened with Carly?? But as Mack turned in the rain and headed for home, he did feel better. The mood was lifting and his body was beginning to ache with the running. He knew that he would sleep soundly.

Ironically he was soaked to the skin when he got home. A recent image of being soaked to the skin in Christina's garden flashed through his mind. In the hot shower images of Christina ran through his mind at a much slower pace. No soap but he had shower gel. It would be rude not to honour Christina!!

Mack slept more soundly that night than he could have imagined. It was amazing what something clean but oh so dirty could do!

(79) It's Beginning to Look a Lot Like Christmas

Just like John Rippon had predicted, the garage was really busy. It was if everyone and their aunt wanted a new car in time for the really bad winter weather. Mack felt sure that his shiny chrome truck would be sold, it really was a beauty, but as November ticked into December, possession of the truck keys stayed firmly in his hands.

It had been a bumper month. Mack and the rest of the sales team worked 6 day weeks, until the first week in December when the customers stopped coming as if someone had turned off the tap.

All the extra hours they had worked in the busy period were taken in December, so Mack found that for the first time in forever, he had time on his hands on the run up to the festive period.

Mack had kept in touch with Melissa, work had taken priority and he hadn't seen her for weeks and weeks. But they messaged daily and he did promise her that when things settled down workwise, he would treat her out.

For the first time in a very long time, Mack didn't have any dalliances with any females. It had been all work work work. He found he didn't even have time for the gym, he liked to get into work early and then would stay until everything was done and there was no chance of a customer wandering on to the pitch.

He ran as much as he could. Running wasn't as intrusive as the gym, he literally would get in from work, change into trackies and away he would go. It was a little bit of Mack time, a get down from the hype of the garage. Not that the garage was stressful, Mack could honestly say he was really enjoying his job, but it could be nonstop and he had learned to juggle fast, something his mam had found amusing, she had been juggling since the day he was born she had said.

The weekend before Christmas Len Pearson had arranged a big Christmas Party. It was at a castle and apparently it was where the garage went every year, it was a thank you for all of the hard work his staff had done for him. Hotel rooms were booked and according to everyone, it was the best weekend ever. No one paid a penny, it was all courtesy of Len Pearson Cars.

Mack was looking forward to it. He had been given the opportunity of taking a plus one. But who? He thought about Melissa, she would love a trip away in a castle.

But Mack wasn't sure who would be there, certainly the lovely Mrs Jones would be, but he hadn't really had chance to speak to her with the garage being so busy workwise and his mobile had been devoid of her texts, so whether Mr Jones was back on the scene was still a mystery to him. Best not take Melissa just in case, she didn't deserve that. If Nichola Jones got tipsy and started with her flirtatious behaviour and anything came out, it would be curtains with Melissa. She wasn't daft and would know that if anything had happened with Mrs Jones, it had been since he started there and was therefore it was while he was doing what ever it was he was doing with Melissa.

As selfish as it was, he didn't want to quite give up on Melissa. This period of abstinence he had enforced on himself was giving him a little bit of clarity. He intended to see a bit of her over the festive period, he might even take her home to meet Paula, in his mam's eyes that would be a Christmas Miracle.

But for the Len Pearson Cars Christmas Party, he was just going to fly solo. He wouldn't be the only one there without a significant other half, a couple of the mechanics were single and he was sure he had heard that some of the admin girls where just going on their own, making the most of the spa and pool, but he wasn't sure if that included Nichola Jones or not. Better to be safe than sorry.

Mack was actually feeling content on the run up to that Christmas. He had a bit money in his bank, his credit card balance was manageable and he had some peace of mind, there were no female blockages. He wasn't even jittery that he hadn't had sex in a few weeks, life just seemed easier for some reason.

Becky had been texting him. She had tickets for the Newcastle United game on New Year's Day if he was interested. Mack had stared at his phone for quite some time thinking about his answer. He would like nothing more than going to watch Newcastle play on New Year's Day, what a way to start his year off and so far he hadn't any plans to go out the previous night, so there would be no hang over to nurse. But then there was Becky. What had Becky been about. She had snuck under the covers and made him smile, but that had been weeks ago and he hadn't heard from her since, not until she text about the tickets.

The stupid thing was that he had thought that he would actually be able to have a little go at coupledom over Christmas with Melissa, one text from Becky had seemed to have put all of that in jeopardy, even just in his head. Thoughts of her pixie haircut bopping up and down in the darkness as he lay on her settee was too much. Without a shadow of a doubt Mack would be up for a repeat performance!

Just as he was about to text Becky back, another message pinged through. She had two tickets if he could use them. What was that about. Had she sensed his hesitancy?? No, it had only been a matter of minutes. Two tickets?? They were like gold dust and he would certainly be having them, pixie bopping head or not. New Year's Day at St James

Park was a no brainer, especially if he could take someone with him. 'Yes yes yes thank you thank you thank you!' he text back.

Saying she would see him Christmas Day with details, the deal was done. Christmas Day??? Mack knew nothing about any of that. A question he would be having with Paula. Why hadn't he been told that Tom would be there with his lot on Christmas Day? He would have to get extra presents!

Back on his phone he fired a text off to Marty. Who else?? Somewhere in the depth of his mind he had a feeling that the baby was due at the beginning of December, but couldn't be sure. If Marty couldn't, there would be another mate who would happily use up the spare seat.

(80) Get the Party Started   #pink

By the time he was pulling up his shiny chrome truck in the car park in front of the castle that was to host Len Pearson Cars, Christmas treat, Christmas and New Year was sorted.

Mack had intended to be at the venue much earlier than he actually arrived. He had called at the garage in the morning and had stumbled across someone on the pitch which had ultimately turned into a sale, result. But there had been loose arrangements to make use of the swimming pool there and knew a lot of his colleagues would be arriving early to make most of it.

By the time Mack got to his room he was at an inbetween time, too late to go see if the others were in the pool but too early for the party. So he had himself his second shower of the day and lay on his four poster bed.

The room was really elegant, finished off to the highest of standard, but it was all very dated looking. God knows how old the castle was but everything in the room looked authentic and it gave Mack the willies a bit. How many people had stayed in that room, slept in the bed or died in the room. It didn't smell musty or anything, but it had a distinct smell. Sage or something.

Needing to bring himself back from the days of knights of old, Mack switched on the tv and watched the news while he waited for it to be a decent enough time to get himself dressed and make his way down to the bar where everyone was told to meet at 7pm. Mack was looking forward to spending some time with his workmates, it was a very different to the Call Centre Christmas do's which usually ended up being a riot and they were never allowed to go back to the venue again. If this was what they did every year at the castle, then everyone must be on their best behaviour Mack thought to himself.

He had brought a suit with him, it was navy blue, or was it French blue, anyway it was almost black and he had a pale blue shirt to wear with it. He had brought a couple of ties, he had forgot to ask the lads if they were expected to wear ties, but he would put one on and if no one else was wearing a one he could easily take it off and slip it into his pocket.

Staring at the reflection in the mirror; he was happy at the Mack who stared back at him. The late night runs had done him good; the extra lbs he had packed on had gone and he looked toned in his suit.

No matter what happened, what tasty temptations were laid out before him; he vowed that there would be nothing going bump in the night in his room.

Just before 7 he made his way down to the bar where everyone was meeting. He would rather be there to greet people that make an entrance on his own; but entering the bar area, it seemed to be something all the 'soloists' had thought to do; it was already quite full.

There was an open bar; Mack would never imagine that happening at the Call Centre; it would have been drunk dry within the first hour. They had always been given something that looked like poker chips; each one would be the value of one drink; they were never given more that three each. So ordering a drink at the bar and not paying for it felt a very alien experience.

Soon the whole area began to fill up as the staff from Len Pearson Cars and their better halves began to arrive.

Justin arrived with Amelia; who looked stunning in her evening dress. Making for Mack the three of them were soon joined By Kevin; his wife Joanne, Craig and Sean. When John Ripon and his wife Laura the little group of sales people was complete and with all the chat going on between them; Mack didn't have chance to see who else was at the Christmas party until the gong rang out summoning the party to the great hall and their dinner.

As happened on such occasions; the sales team who worked together every day, sometimes 6 days a week; sat together.

Mack felt a bit of an odd one out and thought to himself that maybe he should have brought Melissa with him after all; there was no threat on their table about any thing that Mack had got up to.

But a quick glance around the room and Mack knew he had done the right thing.

Mr and Mrs Jones were taking their seats at the next table. Mrs Jones saw Mack looking and smiled. It was one of those smiles. One of those smiles that only people who have previously been intimate can share.

She looked stunning and Mack hoped that he would have opportunity to tell her; if not that night then he would go out of his way to tell her on Monday.

Mr Jones was a lucky man. He looked like he knew he was lucky. He was holding his wife's hand and kissing it; Mack wondered if underneath his shirt was he covered in bites and scratches. Mrs Jones; the vixen. If Mr and Mrs Jones were back together on a permanent footing; Mack was pleased for them.

One of the valeters; Dean jumped in the unoccupied seat next to Mack. He was pleased to see him; he didn't like to feel like a spare part. Dean's wife had only recently had a baby so Dean was flying solo too. He made Mack laugh when he said he was pleased she had decided she wasn't coming; previous years she always ended up dancing on the tables and making a proper tit of herself.

Just as the starters were about to be served; Len Pearson came to their table to say hello, very dapper in dinner suit and dickie bow tie; he looked every inch the boss.

Promising the ladies at the table a spin around the dance floor later when the music started; he left them to their starters.

Mack watched to see where he was seated. Which of the Pearsons were at his table.

But it was a fruitless exercise; wherever it was that Len Pearson was sitting was way out of eyeshot; Mack could make out Len sitting down, but the rest of his companions remained a mystery.

(81) Proud Mary   #tinaturner

It was good banter around the table. The wine flowed and Mack found that he was really enjoying himself. Good food and good company. Craig was the star of the show; happy to have an audience; his campness was on overdrive.

With the dessert dishes cleared away; the band came on and the dance floor filled.

Mack was happy to sit on his seat and observe.

Craig was in the middle of the admin girls strutting his stuff; Mack wished he could be a bit less himself and a bit more like Craig; he only danced when he was drunk and even though he was merry; he wasn't at the couldn't give a shit phase.

But the band were good and certainly knew how to get the dance floor filled.

Having eventually having to go and break the seal, Mack was on his way back from the gents when he saw her.

She was walking back from the bar; a flute of something in each hand. She saw him too; there was a look. Mack wasn't sure what it was; maybe appreciation, no not appreciation, more like satisfaction. She looked like the cat that got the cream.

It gave Mack a funny tingling feeling. She was something else.

Wearing a full length black dress that clung to her body; hair was piled on top of her head and without even having to look, Mack could tell that she was in stiletto heels.

Something was stirring in Mack; and it wasn't his stomach with the food and drink. The stirrings were further south than his stomach.

He made his way back to his seat and Dean. Who was busy recording something on the dance floor on his phone. Craig! Who at the time was doing a very fine impression of Tina Turner as the band belted out Proud Mary.

Shaken and stirred. Mack did the only thing he could do; poured himself a big glass of wine and gulp it down like he would a pint.

And then another and another and then he was up on the dance floor strutting his stuff with Craig and the rest of the staff from Len Pearson Cars who seemed to be as pissed as he was.

The band finished and the disco started and for the rest of the night he did a run backwards and forwards from the table to drink his wine and the dance floor.

(82) Table for Two   #yxngbane

The hangover was probably one of the worst he had ever had.

Worst still was he had great big chunks of the night missing.

He awoke in the creepy room and had no idea where he was. He was still dressed in his suit but under the bed covers. The one good thing was that he was alone in the room; he hadn't done anything daft.

But still. He had no idea if he had made a tit of himself.

Mack spent a long time in the shower; the safest place for him seeing as he thought he might be sick. The wine had been a bad idea. He knew when he was drinking it that he should have just swerved it; it never did him any favours.

Dressed and looking much more decent than he felt; he made his way down to the restaurant for breakfast.

Expecting to find the place packed with his work colleagues; he was surprised to find only one or two of them, who looked as rough as he felt.

Ordering himself coffee and a full English; he sat himself on a table that looked onto the vast gardens. He really had no idea how the evening ended. Not as bad as it could have; but still. He really didn't like not to have any control over situations and with all the missing bits; he had no idea what had happened. Especially with her there.

As if by thinking of her somehow magically manifested her; there she was sitting herself down on the seat opposite her.

She looked and smelt amazing. If she had drank copious amounts of alcohol; then she certainly wasn't carrying it the next morning; then Mack didn't look like he was either; the only thing he felt now the nausea had passed was his brain; which seemed to have shrunk to the size of a pea; rattling around in his head.

They made small talk.

Yes it had been a good night. The meal had been delicious. The band were really good.

To Mack it seemed that he had not spoken to her at all the night before. Phew; he hadn't made a tit of himself.

If he had spoken to her and she wasn't in his bed when he woke up; she hadn't rejected him. That was one saving Grace.

Relaxing and sipping on his coffee which at first he thought was going to make him feel sick again; they chit chatted.

Yes she came to the Christmas Do every year.

No she hadn't finished her Christmas shopping.

The mindless chatter went on and all the time they spoke; Mack took her in.

It was the first time he'd had chance to have a proper look at her. Obviously he had been up close and personal with her; but that had been in a haze of lust. This was just two people over breakfast.

She was pretty. Very pretty. But there was an edge about her. Mack liked it. It was like he could look but not touch, a bit of aloofness. In

Mack's experience girls looked at him and had a wantness about them. Like they encourage him. She was different. It would be her terms or the highway. Mack really liked it. It was his thing.

The stirring in Mack's southern region was back. Thankfully his breakfast arrived; closely followed by hers and the conversation went back onto an even keel and all was well again in the south.

By the time they had finished their breakfast; the restaurant had filled up and there were lots of people stopping off at their table; many who had about the same amount of memory as Mack and wanted him to fill in their blank points. A good night seemed to be had by all.

And then she was gone.

Mack kicked himself for not asking for her mobile number. He was losing his touch.

As he watched her walk out of the restaurant, he felt gutted.

He looked away; wouldn't do for his workmates to look at him sitting with his tongue hanging out; especially as they had already been giving him knowing looks when they found them together, sharing a table and eating their breakfast.

If only; Mack had thought to himself.

(83) 12 Days of Christmas #perrycomo

The one good thing was that he would still be able to have Christmas with Melissa. He hadn't done anything wrong. He had gone to his Christmas Party; got drunk and by all accounts hadn't even kissed another girl.

Coupledom was still an option for him.

Then again, Mack thought not. He had managed to have instantaneously hard ons' just looking at her. It hadn't happened often to him. Stacey's Mom's texts had done it, Jude Johnson and her photos; Christine in her skimpy gardening attire. Usually it took more.

She was more. Much more just being herself.

She was something else.

But she was gone. Again.

It was a lively run up to Christmas.

At work cars continued to sell. It was slightly bucking the trend of previous years where December had tended nose dive. No one was complaining though; it wasn't very Ho Ho Ho, but they all just got on with it not really knowing when the tap would be turned back off.

Mack saw a lot of Melissa; she loved to shop and would happily trail around the shops with Mack; another new thing, usually he would just shop online the week before and then panic that nothing would turn up.

And when Marty rang to tell Mack that Dina had given birth to a baby girl; Melissa had gone with him to Marty's house to see his best friend's new edition.

It was a bit of a pre-coupledom period.

It had all the whistles and bells of being in a proper relationship, just without the parents.

Mack was on his best behaviour.

There were no distractions. Mrs Jones was with Mr Jones and even though to all intents and purposes nothing had changed since he had gone to work there; she still flirted with him outrageously; that was all it was. They had got close; very close, but no one knew and Mack was glad about that. Nichola Jones could go and skip happily into the sunset with her husband. There was no harm done; infact if anything the whole little thing they'd had actually aided the reconciliation with her husband.

A bit marriage guidance .

Mack was happy for her.

So there was no immediate distraction at work. Mack was friendly with the rest of the female staff there, but there was none that would take him off his road to a relationship of sorts with Melissa.

She really was very nice.

Melissa may not have had that thing that Mack liked; but she had assets in other areas and if he had learned anything over the past few years, it wasn't all about the sex.

Mack could never imagine that Melissa would be a Stacey's Mom; she didn't really wear the stilettos for a start and the thought of her demanding anything of Mack seemed an unlikely thing for Mack to put on his Christmas list. But they still had a good time; in and out of the bed.

Paula would love Melissa and the thought of taking her home did cross through his head. But it was still early days; he had cheated on her so many times; well not cheated; they weren't official. It didn't say that they were in a relationship on Facebook for a start. And he didn't want to build up anyone's hopes; Melissa's or Paula's.

But it was something else too. Mack's mam; Paula and Tom's family were all having Christmas together. This included Becky who had so wrongly taken advantage after the cup game at Newcastle.

It just wouldn't be fair on Melissa. Or Mack, or Becky.

There had been nothing from pixie like Becky since the match apart from the news of the tickets for the New Year's Day match and there had certainly been no mention of what had happened in the wee hours of the morning when he had stayed at Becky's house.

No Melissa could be a visitor for the New Year.

She hadn't asked about seeing him and she hadn't invited him over to hers.

On a whim and because his wages had included a bonus that made a difference; Mack booked New Year's Eve at a swanky hotel in Northumberland; the whole kit and caboodle for him and Melissa.

And then gave himself an imaginary pat on the back for even thinking about seeing the New Year in with Melissa. It might have been a small step towards coupledom, but it was a step forward.

When Marty asked him to go and see the new baby; Mack took Melissa.

The look on Marty's face said it all.

Mack said nothing; just introduced Melissa to Marty; Dina and Reggie and then waited for them to be introduced to Belle; their newest addition.

As much as Mack tried to play it down to himself; taking Melissa to meet Dina and Marty was a big thing. He hadn't done anything remotely like that since he was with Carly.

Thinking of Carly was like a punch in the stomach. They hadn't been together for ages, but the fact that she was pregnant had really selfishly shook him up.

Could he have been a good dad?? He didn't know. He would have said that Marty would have been crap at it; mainly because he had never really seen him with a baby before Reggie came along. He had never really had a steady girlfriend before Dina. It was usually the 7 hour or 7 day or 7 week or if she was really special the 7 month itch with regards to Mack's best friend.

But look at him now!!! He was like Father Time. He handled his babies like he had been doing it all of his life.

There was maybe hope for Mack. Obviously not with Carly; that door was well and truly closed in his face. But someone!

What was a bigger punch in his stomach was that even though he had been thinking about fatherhood and his ability or inability to take to it. He hadn't thought of Melissa as the mother. Just someone.

Force of habit maybe.

(84) Mistletoe and Wine   #cliffrichard

Christmas Eve at Len Pearson Cars was a very jolly affair.

With most of the work done the day previous; it really only remained for the staff to go into work; swap Secret Santa presents; have a drink and then head off to the pub for more drinks. The number of drinks dependent on home commitments; but with little else to do; Mack knew he would be there until the bitter end.

Mrs Pearson had laid on a buffet; she even stayed a while and orchestrated the Secret Santa gifts so that no one knew where the gifts had come from.

Mack had got John Rippon. The man who had everything! A £15 quid limit was a big ask, but Melissa; Bless her had suggested a tie. A bit safe, but to be fair, John hardly knew him so it seemed like as good an idea as anyone. But it had been a funky one and something different to what John Rippon usually wore; it would probably never see the light of day.

Mack hated Secret Santa; years of them in the Call Centre had always resulted in him receiving something embarrassing. The amount of packets condoms and lube he had got in Christmas's past was ridiculous. And as much as a Jack the Lad he was; it made him a nervous wreck every time the event came around.

Hopefully the staff at Len Pearson Cars who had pulled his name out of the cup had no idea of the persona that he had earned when he was in the Call Centre. But still. He was dreading it.

As much as he dreaded it. It happened and then was over.

A tie! It seemed that he must have fell into the same category as John Rippon. If in doubt; get them a tie. It was a nice tie though; and he knew he would wear it. Turned out the whole sales team got them.

But at least it wasn't condoms and lube!

Mack made most of the buffet. If he was heading off to the pub, God knows when he would eat again. And it really was a nice buffet. Mrs Pearson had gone to great lengths.

And then it was time to lock up the garage; until Boxing Day anyway; Mack would be back in to work the Bank Holiday; it was the only way he would have been able to get New Years Day off which allegedly was always a good selling day for the garage; but Mack wanted to go to the match so would just have to miss out of the bonanza.

The pub was good. It was one that Mack had never been in to before; it was a bit classier than the one they usually went to after work, which was a bit spit and sawdust.

And there was a good mix of people too. Mrs Jones was there; only staying for one she said to Mack as she stood beside him at the bar. They had a funny relationship; Mack liked it.

They had that layer to them that only people who had been intimate could have. Mr Jones had moved back in and although he still hadn't found a permanent job, he had signed up with an agency and was starting a job in the new year. It was all that he needed to do Mrs Jones said. Make an effort. And so Mr and Mrs Jones were an item again and she looked radiant. Not that she hadn't when she was single, but marriage obviously suited her better.

The drinks flowed and one by one people began to leave. Each being kissed and wished all the best blah blah blah as only you can do at Christmas.

Len Pearson left, but not before getting his staff one last round of drinks in. Mack really liked him; he was old school but knew that if he kept his staff happy they would work hard. Not like some of the management at the Call Centre who thought that ridiculing staff and putting them down was a better management ploy. The turnover of staff at the Call Centre was phenomenal; getting beating with a sharp stick didn't work. His mam had a saying; 'you get more with sugar than you do shit'. Mack thought that was probably one of Len Pearson's mantras too, he certainly had happy staff.

In the end there was just Mack, Kevin, the two mechanics called Andrew, Vicky from accounts and a couple of admin girls that Mack couldn't remember what they were called.

The drinks continued to flow and it seemed that none of them were in a rush to get home. Kevin said he was in no hurry; Christmas Eve was Craig and his mam's night, they wore matching pyjamas drank Baileys and got everything ready for the following day.

Mack couldn't imagine him and Paula wearing matching pyjamas; even back in the day when there had just been the two of them. But each to their own.

Considering it was Christmas Eve, the pub was packed.

Mack did think about dropping Melissa a text to come and join him, but they had already exchanged small gifts; Mack's being in a card with the news of their night away on New Year's Eve; it was personal without being personal. Coupledom was still an option but with his recent form;

Mack just couldn't give Melissa the wrong impression by buying her something personal; he wasn't out of the wood yet and onto the road sign posted monogamy.

So he let sleeping dogs lie and left Melissa to her Christmas Eve plans.

By the time that last orders was called; Mack was quite drunk. Not the falling over type; just the type that kissed Kevin on the lips when he left for home and that although he had no interest in the two girls that worked in admin; he was flirting with them.

To be honest; if he had been working at the Call Centre and so had they; he would have chanced his luck. They seemed to be good friends and he was sure if he went full out Mack Attack; he could have got them both in to bed. Together!

But he had nowhere to take them if the truth be known. Paula would have been furious if he had taken them back to theirs; it would have to be back to one of the girls and they didn't look like the type that had their own pad. No, sneaking out of some random's family house in the wee hours of Christmas Day just wasn't his style anymore.

And then there was work. What would people say. It hadn't so much mattered in the past, but things were different now. He had a proper job with proper people; he didn't want news of his shenanigans reverberating throughout the building. He had sailed close to the wind already there. And it had only been by sheer luck rather than good management that word hadn't got out about Elle and the casting couch interview; Mrs Jones or Jenny Coates and the test drive.

Just the thought of all the near misses sobered him up and he fired off a message to the one woman he couldn't do without.

Paula; his mam.

Within half an hour she was pulled up outside the pub. If she was annoyed about picking him up she didn't seem it; it had been a long time since he had put in a mercy call for his mam to come and collect him because he couldn't get a taxi. But it had been a good day and after wishing everyone a Merry Christmas; Mack was on his way home having done nothing to dent the halo that was starting to glow above his head.

(85) Merry Xmas Everybody   #slade

Christmas Day turned out to be a very busy one at Mack's.

Firstly it had been him and his mam sitting around the tree opening their gifts; Melissa had got him tickets to see Sam Fender the following year. There was two in the card; if it was a gift for the two of them; she had given him control of the tickets; 6 months was a long time. A big commitment for both of them. 6 days was a big commitment for Mack! But it was a lovely gift and Mack fired off a text to her thanking her and wishing her a Merry one.

Paula was sitting with raised eyebrows. It seemed like an awfully big gift from a girl she had never met she said. Mack said she was a work in progress but to watch that space.

His granddad arrived not long after they got up; he didn't like Christmas much without Mack's nan so had thought it would be better if he was around people and not sitting in his own house feeling sorry for himself.

Paula rushed around the house getting the dinner ready and the table dressed and hoovering; she was like a mad woman. Tom and his mam and the girls were coming as well as Auntie Lynn and Uncle Peter, though Mack's cousins wouldn't be showing their face this year, which made Mack a bit sad. It was tradition.

Tom arrived with his mam; Nancy; and Lucy. Becky he said was hoping to make it there in time for lunch but they had training that morning and she wouldn't be able to stay long as she was heading off to meet up with the team for their match in Leicester the following day. Mack was once again impressed with Becky!

But she was there by the time everyone sat around the table.

Paula had really gone full out. There was a little scratch card for everyone in the champagne flute and Mack thought he was the only lucky one winning £2 until he checked his granddad's and he had won £100.

Mack tried his best not to look at Becky. He could still remember what had happened at her house the night he slept on the couch. But she didn't seem to be phased about Mack being there and chatted about how the team were doing; who had slight injuries which would need to be worked on before the following day and how the big signing they had made the previous summer and had only managed to play one game was fighting fit again and hoping to at least make it onto the bench for the next match.

And Mack was hooked again.

She was one of the most interesting women he had ever met. Probably because of her job; would he had thought her half as fascinating if she was an ice hockey team's physio?? Probably not. But she wasn't she worked for Newcastle United and that made her something very special in Mack's book.

As Christmas Day's went; it was a good one. The conversation had flowed over their meal; obviously Becky held court a lot; which was only right and considering everyone around the table was a football fan; she was interesting.

Becky and Lucy left not long after their meal.

But for the rest of the day, everyone was content to sit and watch shit telly; have a few drinks and eat chocolates.

Mack's granddad took Tom's mam; Nancy home; Auntie Lynn and Uncle Peter set off home and when it was just the three of them left; Mack retreated to his room to watch more shit on his telly; drink a couple of beers and get himself ready for work the next day.

Melissa text; just general stuff but she was over the moon that they were going away for New Year and had even bagged herself a killer dress she said in the sales that had started on Christmas Day. Better still her mam and dad had surprised her with 2 weeks holidays in Florida at Easter. It was a big family thing and sounded very exciting.

Mack couldn't think of anything worse than going to America!

The trip with Carly to Las Vegas that had never happened had put him off all things American for life.

As tempted as he was; he refrained from searching Carly out on Facebook; he was still a Facebook friend with her; but had set his account so he didn't get any of her posts. The thought of her showing off her baby bump dressed as a Christmas Pudding or something would be too much. He was a fool. It could have been him. But the damage had been done and it was a big lesson learnt.

Or was it! If his recent conduct was anything to go by then he thought not. Melissa was a good one; she was holding his attention; mainly. She may even turn out to have that thing that really held his attention with time. Mack thought not though; she was too wholesome; too nice. As if that should even be a problem; most people would give their right hand to have a girl that doted on them; that was pretty and loyal and kind and clever.

Not Mack though; it didn't seem to be in his DNA and that made Mack feel a little bit on the glum side as he turned off his telly; knocked off the light and reached down into his boxers. It had been Jude Johnson that had scuppered his trip to America; but she had been something else and just thinking back to his cheating ways with her had woken up his sleeping wee Mack; it would be a little while yet before he would be in the land of nod.

(86) Auld Lang Syne

By the time he was picking Melissa up to drive to the hotel where they would be spending their New Year's Eve; it had been a very busy week in the garage.

True to form; the customers had arrived and the cars had sold. It had been a great end to his first Christmas at Len Pearson Cars. His January bonus would be a really good one and he was pleased with himself. Despite his lack of experience in car sales; he had held his own with the rest of the Sales Team and John Rippon had said he would not have been more pleased with his team before they had left the garage for the New Year Celebrations.

Mack still had the truck and it was an absolute joy driving out into the countryside in it with a very giddy Melissa sitting in the passenger seat.

It was a very 'couple' thing to be doing. Mack quite liked it.

The hotel was as lavish as it looked on their website. It still had all the sparkle of Christmas with the added glitz of New Year's Eve.

Their room looked out into the grounds; it was stunning and to celebrate Melissa and Mack showered together; then used every surface of their room for what ever took their fancy. Melissa was very bendy. It was nice to have some where that wasn't the back of the truck or Melissa's mam and dad's house. Melissa seemed to let herself go a bit more and Mack appreciated the fact.

It turned out to be a really good night. The food; the drink; the bands that the hotel had laid on for their guest and the dress that Melissa wore clung to her lithe like body like a skin. Mack liked that she continuely got admiring glances; not just off men, but women too. She really was a good looking girl.

As the bells chimed midnight; Mack kissed Melissa like she was the only girl in the world for him. Which she was. He even sent up a silent promise to the big man in the sky that he would be better. That the beautiful girl that he was with would be his one and only.

But it wasn't to last.

It had been one of the best nights Mack'd had for a very long time.

But the next day was match day.

(87) Going Home   #markknopler

A New Year; it was certainly a more positive outlooked Mack who jumped into his best mates car and headed off into the city.

Usually the most he had looked forward to each New Year; certainly the ones since him and Carly had split up; was his annual holiday which would usually be about 6 months on the horizon.

That New Year he had a job he loved; a sort of girlfriend and an eye on what he could achieve if he continued to work hard at Len Pearson Cars. It was a good feeling and now it was match time with his best mate; he was a happy soul.

Marty was in good spirits too. The new baby was well and Reggie had taken to his baby sister. Mack was unsure why he wouldn't have; but just agreed with his mate that yes it was a good thing. Mack knew as much about babies as he had about cars when he had got the job at Len Pearson Cars.

Over a pint before the game; Marty filled Mack in about the Christening. Reggie and Belle were going to be baptised at Easter and Mack was still to be Reggie's godfather. Mack filled Marty in on his big toe foray into coupledom with Melissa and how so far he had kept everything well and truly in his pants. Well apart from Becky he had said; his step-sister in waiting who had sorted the tickets out for the match for them. Marty had laughingly said if it took a blow job to keep them in tickets then he Mack should always just give in.

It turned out to be a great afternoon. Their seats were almost front row and watching another win was icing on the cake. Mack could see Becky down beside the dug out; she looked like one of the blokes and it took

Marty a while to spot her when Mack pointed out the girl who had kindly given them their tickets.

Marty was heading home straight after the match; his mam was at his house helping out with the kids; Marty of old wouldn't have given a shit and would have headed into a pub with Mack; but the new version of Marty needed to get home; you can never be sure when you would need help again he stated; didn't want to take the piss.

But they would stay in the stadium for one until the traffic died down and Mack didn't mind heading home early; he'd had a late night and an early morning himself so a night in the house before work the next day wouldn't do any harm.

Then Becky text!

There was a get together in the function room did they want to go??

Marty was sticking to his guns and heading home; Mack obviously wasn't missing an opportunity to mix with the good people of Newcastle United and of course would love to go. All thoughts of his early night so he could be work ready in the morning well and truly out of the window.

And Mack's good intentions last little over 24 hours.

(88) Shots   **#imaginedragons**

He woke early the next morning in a strange bedroom but with a familiar head of hair; or lack of it; lying on the pillow next to his.

It had been a good night by all accounts.

There had been a few Newcastle players at the 'do', but none of the ones that had played that afternoon; or any he could actually call first team players. But he had spoken to a few old timers from back in the day when he had gone to the matches with his mam or his mates and he recognised a few local pundits and reporters. But it had been mainly made up of backroom staff and Becky's work colleagues.

Mack had been pleased he went though.

Well he had up until he woke up that morning and realised that once again the lovely Melissa was out of sight and out of mind.

Somewhere in his hangover fog he could remember being all over Becky.

Not at the 'do! That would have been embarrassing for her and somewhere in the back of his mind he had remembered her telling him that she liked to give all her workmates the idea that she was batting for the other side and was into women. Of course that was just a smoke screen. She just hadn't wanted them putting her into difficult situations and work becoming awkward. She was a very pretty girl.

No it had been later; when they had left St James Park and decided that they would have one for the road before heading off towards their respective homes.

The one for the road had turned into quite a few for many roads. The town was bouncing; it was New Years Day and Newcastle had won their first game of the year and somehow Mack and Becky were buoyed along and before they knew it they were in a crowded club; necking shots and getting very up close and personal on the dance floor.

More shots and more dancing and lots and lots of roaming hands; both Mack and Becky.

It was inevitable that they both got into the same taxi outside of the club and they had barely sat on the back seat when they were all over each other. Becky even managed to get her hand down Mack's jeans before they had finished the 10 minute taxi ride back to her place.

This time there was no sofa sleeping for Mack. The only time that he was on the sofa was while Becky did a repeat performance of his last visit to her house. Once again her little pixie like head bopped up and down as she went to work on Mack. This time there was no finish for him on the sofa. This time she wanted more and boy did she get it.

Becky was small and light and very very fit. Mack was still a little overweight and nowhere near the fitness level he had been before he started in sales. She had him worn out. But he wasn't complaining. He complained less when he saw that her left boob was pierced and when he eventually worked himself between her legs; there were piercings there too. Mack was blown away. He had never encountered a bejazzeled lady area before.

Regrets; he had a few.

Mack certainly regretted drinking as much as he did; he had no idea how he would make it through his working day!

Becky regrets not so much so. He'd had a good time. She certainly didn't appear to be the needy sort. From what he could remember of the night before she had made it quite clear to him that she wasn't expecting anything from him. But he had heard that old chestnut before so time would tell with that one.

Melissa he did have regrets about though. It had been less that 24 hours between Mack dropping her off on New Years Day at her house and Becky dropping Mack off at his.

He was a twat. No two ways about it. But what was done was done.

Mack liked Becky. Not like liked her; but liked her and she was his mam's boyfriend's daughter so wouldn't be disappearing from him life completely, he would remain on good terms with her. And if he was honest he couldn't be sure that what happened wouldn't happen again. It had been an interesting night; he had stirring in the shower when he thought about it. But there was no time for indulging in re-caps of pixie heads and piercings; he had to get to work in record time and he was already running later than he would have liked.

(89) January   #pilot

The only thing he wanted to do was work. He was still relatively new to the trade and had so much to learn. He would channel all his energy into work; keep his nose clean and dodge Melissa for a little while; he couldn't face her. She was sure to ask about the match and he really didn't have the energy or inclination to lie to her. Best to keep himself busy and out of arms reach until New Year's Day became a distant memory and he was back on an even keel.

And that is what he did. He worked as many hours as he could; arranged to see customers on his days off so that he would have an excuse to go in and even rocked up at the garage on a Sunday when he knew that Les Pearson would be working on the pitch.

Melissa took his aloofness for hard work. It would never have crossed her mind that Mack would have a bit of a guilty conscious and was avoiding her. He had told her he was trying to get his monthly bonus up to a decent amount so he could save it towards a place of his own. It was something of the truth; he couldn't stay at his mam's forever; he was a grown man, but he had no intention of moving out anytime soon; he fancied a holiday and if he was going to be living a bachelor type existence; then he wanted to live in something that fit the description and that would be pricey.

So January passed in a haze of work.

Each day Mack's confidence in the job grew and he was loving it. The garage was busy; with the continued winter weather the enquiries were flying in and each enquiry that landed on Mack's desk was an opportunity for a sale. Years and years at the Call Centre calling customers came second nature; where he had seen Justin and even Kevin faulter if they didn't have an idea about what each customer wanted prior to the telephone call; Mack had no such qualms and the proof was in the pudding. The customers came and the cars sold.

Away from work he was still distancing himself from Melissa.

After work he would either go and have a quick pint with whoever had locked up the garage with him; January saw him acting like the factory cat and even if he wasn't the first into the garage in a morning; he would certainly be the last out. So if one of the lads was still there; or even one of the girls; they would head off for a swift one on the way home and by the time he made it through the front door; he would be ready for his bed.

The only other thing that Mack did was the gym.

Back in his Call Centre days he would have been at the gym most days; but since he went into car sales, his visits had slipped and even though he would still play five-a-side with his mates when he could, the gym had sort of gone on the back burner and so had his body.

He could vividly remember how unfit he had felt the night he had spent with Becky. She admitted herself that she worked out most days; being a physio it sort of went with the territory. But Mack hadn't liked it. He had always been it tip top condition since his teens; to a certain extent vain. But nowadays he knew his fitness levels weren't were they should be and he had a small; miniscule roll of fat around the top of his work pants. Mack didn't like it.

Back to the gym he went. When he first went back he almost threw the towel straight in. The place was heaving. All the New Year's resolutioners were out in force and getting on to any of the machinery involved a queue of some sort. But as the month wore on; the queue got less and less as more and more people ditched the gym in favour of a cosy night in by the fire.

As with work the hard work began to pay off, the spare tyre diminished and even though he ate and drank far more than he had ever done at the Call Centre; he controlled it by working out at the gym.

(90) Hey Good Looking   **#hankwilliams**

By February Mack was looking and feeling great again.

He did think of seeing Melissa. They talked on the phone and they messaged each other daily, but his own self enforced punishment for New Years Day held strong. There needed to be enough distance from Becky and Melissa for Mack to be able to even consider that illusive phenonium called coupledom.

But he did miss seeing Melissa and still she happily accepted that he was working really hard and had little or no free time beyond work and the occasional jaunts to the gym. Melissa too was working as much overtime as she could; she was off to America in a matter of months so wanted to take as much money as she could with her; so time was precious to both of them and they made do with their mobiles and the occasional 'sex text' that although Melissa was embarrassed about; Mack thought were tame in comparison to some in his past. But still they did the job and for the whole of January; well if you forgot about the 1st day of January when he had theoretically had two women; he was a good lad.

But then he decided that he wanted a bit of colour and the new sunbed shop in the town centre was just the ticket. It opened early and closed late, so was perfect for Mack and his erratic lifestyle working at the garage and going to the gym.

Just like with his body at the gym quickly getting back into shape. It only took a few sunbeds and his skin was getting to be a nice colour. It made always made him feel better having a tan; his hair was dark and the bluey white skin never looked good with all the almost black body hair; a hint of a tan always looked a treat.

The garage continued to be busy.

The cars inside the garage all had great big red bows on them; entice the men in to buy their women the perfect Valentine's gift. But the whole Valentine's thing was making Mack feel a little anxious. He hadn't seen Melissa for weeks; they were text mates and that was as far as it went for the time being. But she would be expecting something for Valentine's surely and Mack wasn't sure how he felt about that.

He wasn't even sure how he felt about Melissa. He did think that his self-enforced celibacy would enflame something within him for her. But as was with Melissa; out of sight and out of mind. He was such a shit.

To be fair to Melissa; she had never asked to see him. She hadn't even brought up the subject of Valentine's Day and as was with Mack; why hadn't she? Did she not want to be with him??

As Valentine's Day approached he went to the gym more often and hit the sunbeds as much as he could. If Melissa didn't want him then he would make sure that he was looking as good as he could be so someone would.

Even to Mack himself he seemed awkward.

He had cheated on Melissa relentlessly; yet he had the audacity to feel wounded that she hadn't suggested seeing him for Valentine's Day.

(91) Here You Come Again   #dollyparton

With nothing arranged; no word from Melissa apart from a Happy Valentine's Day emoji; Mack had himself a mammoth session in the gym and just made it to the sun bed shop before it closed.

The girl on the desk seemed none too pleased when he asked for 12 minutes worth of tokens; that would take her way over her contracted hours she said and the manager was just going to have to lock up on her own; 'it's Valentines Night and I've got places to be!' she had stated huffily as Mack made his way to the cubicle that had his favourite sunbed in.

Twenty minutes later Mack found himself letting coming out of the cubicle into an empty shop.

Thinking that he would do the decent thing and hang back until the shop was secure; he plonked himself down in the waiting area and waited until the manager came front of shop and he would say that he would wait until the shop was closed; aside from him the place was deserted.

Using the time to scroll through his messages; there were so many group chats that he seemed to be park of; there was always something to catch up with; he didn't hear the manager come out into the front.

But he could smell her; it was the distinct smell of Chanel No.5 perfume that always managed to transport him back to a time when he was a young buck and he had a dalliance with one of his friends mams' She was one of his 'it' girls; one of the ones that knew how to make him putty in her hands; and it had only happened a few times in his life despite all of the females that he had slept with; or more to the point had sex with.

Christine; Marty's older neighbour come babysitter; Jude from the Call Centre who had magnificently split him up with Carly; Elle Pearson; his bosses daughter; Elle's friend whose name he couldn't remember when she had come to test drive a car and then of course there had been his friend Stacey's Mom.

It had been Stacey's Mom who would forever more be remember whenever Mack got a waft of Chanel No.5 perfume.

Like then; sitting in the waiting area of the sunbed shop.

Stacey's Mom!

'Fuck!' Mack muttered; unsure if he had said it out loud or just in his head. Because there standing in front of him was Stacey's Mom!

'Fuck indeed!!!' Disadvantaged because he was sitting down; Mack actually thought that he was staring at her with his mouth open and his tongue hanging out.

It must have been over ten years since he had seen her last; longer probably and even though she looked older; the look on her face and her whole persona made the sweaty beast in his boxer shorts almost stand to attention.

'I thought it was you when I saw you on the cameras, but wasn't sure. You're certainly a big lad now Mack! Do you want to come this way?

With that she turned on her very high heels and headed towards the back of the shop!

Mack was powerless.

The hard on in his pants was pointing him in Stacey's Mom's direction; all Mack could do was follow.

Mack was surprised to find that it wasn't an office but some sort of treatment room.

'Take your pants off and lie back on there!'

He was putty! And did as he was told.

For the next 20 minutes Mack felt like he was on of his 'wank bank fantasies!'

Stacey's Mom stripped down to her underwear; which was surprisingly a red teddy thing which most people didn't wear every day Had she been expecting him?? But with the addition of her heels she looked like some sort of porn star; and boy did she act it.

She must have been her fifties; but she seemed to be as fit as pixie haired Becky; she had taken him in her hands and then in her mouth and all the time; whenever Mack had tried to touch her; his hands were pushed away. He was her plaything and how he loved her for it.

In the end she had climbed onto the treatment bed and straddled him.

Reversing so all he could see was her back; she rode him as if he was a rodeo bull. Sensing that she was near coming and unsure that she would finish him off if she came before he did; he let loose, not that it had taken much doing; he could quite easily have come in his boxer shorts in the waiting area a few minutes earlier.

But his release seemed to mark hers and within moments they had both got what they wanted.

Stacey's Mom was fully dressed by the time Mack had put his own clothes back on.

Not a word was spoken.

Mack walked to the front of the shop; waited outside while she closed and locked the door; held back while she let the shutters down and then stood and gawped at her retreating figure as she turned heel and walked away without another word.

Mack had been used and abused once again by Stacey's Mom; and he loved it.

(92) Girl Friend   #avrillavigne

Stacey's Mom was all consuming; any thought of having something stable with Melissa was out of the window. Two women in two month and neither of them were named Melissa.

Once again he threw Melissa back to the Gods. Whereas they would ring and message every day; every day became every other day and they every couple of days and by the end of February; they were barely communicating.

Mack felt bad. He once again used work as an excuse for his absence and infrequent contact; when they did chat he was the same as always even though he knew that all he was doing was letting her down gently. He was never going to be able to have a one on one relationship with her; he couldn't stay faithful to her for five minutes never mind a lifetime.

But in truth he was working hard. The garage was busy; there was always a steady stream of enquiries and with each one it brought a potential sale.

Mack actually loved his job.

He really liked his workmates. Kevin was a hoot and so knowledgeable; especially when he got his eye on a part ex that Mack may be brining in, something for his classic collection. Justin was already just like on of his mates; he had even promised him that the next time that he got tickets for a Newcastle game he would see if he could get one for Justin too. And even John Rippon was all right. Once he had realised that Mack was more than a pair of trousers and a smile and had the makings of a really good car salesman; he went out of his way to help.

Mack felt a bit sorry for John Rippon; he had recently been diagnosed with Osteoporosis; he was only in his mid-forties and John had taken the news badly. If he had once had thoughts about taking over the helm at Len Pearson Cars; which now that Mack knew the business better; seemed like a logical thing for Len Pearson to do when it was time for him to retire; John Rippon would need all the help and support he could get.

Then there were the rest of the staff. Nichola Jones was still a great friend to Mack; they would sometimes have a coffee together in the kitchen and if it was quiet; Mack would run his life past her. Because they had once been close, he felt like her could trust her; it had been Nichola's idea to put some distance between him and Melissa. Even from the outside looking in; Nichola said that she would never hold his attention; he would always cheat on her.

It was the first time in a very long time he had a girl for a friend. Probably since he had stopped being Carly's friend and became her boyfriend. It was nice and sometimes not so nice to get a female perspective of himself; and Nichola was brutally honest.

Mack had told her about Stacey's Mom! Nichola had loved the idea that a woman had actually used him. A refreshing change she had said. But for Mack it had been more than that. And he had even tried to explain to Nichola that it was only the 'it' girls that he ever really wanted more of; obviously present company excepted. But none of the 'it' girls never really wanted him.

And wise old Nichola basically said that after he had distanced himself from Melissa; maybe he should have some time to himself. Not make himself promises he could never keep. Work hard and see what happened next. But not do things just because they were expected of him; like having a steady girlfriend.

She was right. As much as he had loved spending time doing couple type things with Melissa; he was kidding himself if he thought that it was going to lead him into the sunset with her. How many times had he cheated on her. She was so lovely; on paper she ticked all of the boxes; good looking; kind; faithful. He himself only ticked 2/3 boxes and that wasn't good enough.

If he was doomed to be a single lad then he was going to have to put some roots of his own down; he couldn't stay at his mam's house forever.

But after Stacey's Mom, he did take a good long look at himself.

Yes he was tall, dark and handsome. He had a wicked sense of humour and he loved who he loved; his mam and granddad and mates and so on and so forth. He had thought he had loved Carly but that hadn't been enough. There was and had always been that someone else.

But his looks would fade; he was already hurtling towards his thirties; well not exactly hurtling, but they were on the distant horizon. He was still acting like a teenager where women were concerned. Easy come; excusing the pun; and easy go! Quick and cheap thrills.

One day he probably wouldn't have the same pulling power. He would end up being a caricature of a car salesman; sleazy and a little bit creepy!

And that thought scared the shit out of him.

(93) Marry Me   #ollymurs

Once again his sunny disposition dulled and a small storm cloud was hanging over his head. Very out of character but not unknown to him. He was human after all and no one likes a character assassination; even when it's a one you have done to yourself.

All he could do was burn off the negative energy; so he continued to work hard; worked even harder at the gym and kept up the sunbed sessions in the hope that one night the manager would be locking up and there would be a repeat performance of the treatment on the treatment chair.

She was never there though. Mack took slight offence at her absence. Maybe he wasn't as good as he thought he was; but if there was a lack in his performance it was down to her; she was the one that took control and wouldn't let Mack be Mack. He wouldn't let that get him down; he had enough negative forces without adding Stacey's Mom to the list.

There was some good news though. Something that Mack had never thought in a million miles that would happen. Tom had asked his mam to marry him and Paula had said yes. Mack couldn't quite believe it. Obviously Tom was a permanent feature in Paula's life; but he had always thought that they were happy plodding as they were; a few times a week and the odd holiday. But no. They were going to get married and Paula was going to move into Tom's flat and there befell Mack's first bit of good news. Something that made the storm clouds a little bit less stormy!

First the wedding though. Cyprus nonetheless. In June! Mack was impressed with his mam and Tom when they told him all of the good news. They even had links to the venue on their mobiles! Mack was actually excited. They were all going to go for 7 days; or whatever time they could get, but Mack assured Paula that he would be there for the whole duration. Even his granddad was going to go; he had told Paula that there was no way he would allow anyone else to give his only daughter away.

It was hoped that all of the family would go. Tom's too and as Tom said this; Mack had a vision a little pixie head and a wealth of piercings; covered in sun tan oil and sporting an insy wincy teeney weeny bikini! Could be a fun time all around.

Beside the exciting thought of Cyprus in June; his mam flabbergasted him by saying that while she was happy to go and live in Tom's flat with him when they were married; she didn't want to sell the house; she had worked so hard to firstly get a mortgage and then pay the mortgage off. It had been the only home that she and Mack had ever lived in together and one day she said; it would be Mack's anyway.

But in the meantime; if he wanted to, he could live there. There were only a few more years left to pay on the mortgage and the amount was less that anything Mack would pay in rent anywhere else. If he wanted to; Paula would take the mortgage payment off Mack in a monthly payment and he could live in the house.

Mack and his already emotional and maybe even fragile state could feel tears pricking at the back of his eyes as his mam and Tom sat and told him the additional piece of news after the wedding.

Would he like to live in his mam's house??

Of course he would; it was a no brainer!!!

The even paying the mortgage and the bills that went with the house could easily be covered with his basic pay; he had no car costs to pay and beside his gym membership and he now ever depleting balanced credit cards; he had no other outgoings. With his bonus he should and would be able to redecorate the house and make it more in to a 'bachelor's' home!

It wasn't going to be happening straightaway; the wedding was still a few months away; but he would work hard and save as much money as he could so he could be all stations go when his mam made her move, even paying a holiday with all the trimmings in Cyprus!

The storm clouds were definitely beginning to lift. Not just the house, but that his mam was so happy!!

Good things do come to those who wait…

And then he got the text!!!

(94) Feeling Hot Hot Hot   #themerrymen

All the text said was '10pm'

Mack didn't have the contact saved in his mobile but he didn't need to. He was certain that it was Stacey's Mom and the twitch in his boxers somehow confirmed it.

He would be going to the sunbed shop anyway; if it wasn't her then there was no harm done; but there was a fair chance that it was her and he certainly didn't want to miss out on that delight.

So after locking up the garage; he ducked out of a pint with John; headed to the gym where he burned off as much sexual energy as he could; had a shower and then headed off to top up his tan in good time for his 10pm rendezvous.

It was a different receptionist from the one on Valentine's night; still as surely as the first but because it was a little early; she had less attitude handing over the tokens allowing Mack to use up the last minutes of the shop being open.

Lying on the sunbed; Mack tried not to think that somewhere in the building Stacey's Mom was waiting in lure for him. He hadn't spotted her on his arrival but that didn't mean that she wasn't lurking in some back room somewhere and had watched his arrival on the cameras.

Just the thought of her had his pecker perked up.

Certain that there were no cameras in the booth; Mack reached his hand down and into his boxers and felt how excited he was. He had taken a shower at the gym; but he had some wipes in his gym bag and would give himself a little wipe down before he got his clothes back on; and he had aftershave; a little splash of that wouldn't harm. Just in case the 'text for ten' led to something very tasty indeed.

Leaving the cubicle; the waiting area was deserted; it looked like the girl had left for the night; the neon sign that hung next to the door was off as were the window lights. Having an idea that maybe Stacey's Mom was watching him on the cameras; he flung down his gym bag on one of the settees and headed in the direction of the 'treatment' room where he had been treat so badly the last time.

There was a dim light shining under the door; before even opening it Mack knew that Stacey's Mom was inside.

This time it was her on the treatment table.

Mack once again felt like he was drooling from the mouth with his tongue hanging out.

What was before him was a sight of pure perfection.

Stacey's Mom lying on the treatment chair wearing only a black bra; knickers, the French type which always did it for Mack; stockings; suspenders and little ankle boots.

There was no smile to greet him. Just clipped orders telling him what to do; where to touch her; how to do it; how long for.

It was such a turn on.

Half an hour later he was once again watching her walk away from him down the street. He had no idea if he would ever see her again. But for now it didn't matter; all he could think of was the sight of her on the treatment bed; the taste of her and how she made him feel. He was putty; pure and simple.

(95) Hanging on the Telephone   #blondie

Even though he had her number; Mack would never contact her; that would be a big turn off for her he was sure; she liked the control thing and he liked her to have it. If he made contact he would appear to be needy; that wouldn't do. She would punish him by cutting him back out of her life. Too high a price to pay for Mack!

So he waited; he didn't even up his sunbed regime; even if she was there he thought she would ignore him if it hadn't been instigated by her. The first time had been a fluke; she had seen him in the shop and re-ignited the fire; just like when she had seen him in a pub all those years earlier.

The best Mack could do was wait; in hope.

Work was as busy as ever. Craig and Dean were getting married in the summer; not long after his mam, so all talk was of Hag parties and wedding plans; just like at home; his mam might have been going to be an older bride, but she had never been a bride before and Mack was happy to spend some time with her; looking at dresses and clothes for her to take away with her. He quite enjoyed it; she had never been big on getting stuff for herself; it had always been about what Mack wanted and needed.

Melissa seemed to be belonging to the Gods. There had been a few messages and then there was none. Mack felt like a prize shit; she really was lovely. But he didn't think about her 24/7 like he did with Stacey's Mom after an encounter. It would take days and days before he could manage to get her to the back of his mind. Then just as he thought that that was that; there would be a text. The same crack with the time and Mack would be enthralled all over again. She was addictive!

The storm clouds had lifted though. His mood was buoyant again; work was busy and lucrative; each month that passed saw an increase in his bonus; John Rippon was pleased with his progress; Mack seemed to have picked things up; help was something that wasn't a constant now and this allowed the whole sales team to plough ahead full steam. They made a good team.

Len Pearson had made a point of telling them how very pleased he was with them as the financial year ended and a new one began; he had even been good enough to give them all a rise in their basic salary; not a mammoth one but enough to show them how appreciated they were.

Much to Mack's disgust; Justin sold Mack's shiny truck. He had been using it so long he somehow thought he laid claim to it and it was with a heavy heart that he handed over the keys to the mechanics so that they could prepare it for its departure.

After that Mack decided that he would just use whatever vehicle was available; he didn't want to get attached again and to be honest he liked driving different cars; it gave him an idea of what they were capable of and when a customer asked he could give them an honest answer.

Becky had got him tickets for a few more matches; Mack always took them and if Marty couldn't make it then he would take Justin and had even taken his mam on one occasion.

There had been no dalliances with Becky.

With the news of her dad and his mam getting married they had stepped back from one another and acted more like mates than people who had been up close and personal a few times.

It was easier that way.

But he remained at Stacey's Mom's beck and call. She was like a drug and he was an addict.

He knew she would loose interest though; she had the last time. Beyond the sex there was nothing. All Mack had to show for it was his tan which he told everyone was in preparation for Craig's Hag party in Benidorm and his mam's wedding in Cyprus.

If the truth be told he was feeling better than he had in a long time. The gym sessions had helped not just with his body but also his mind. The storm clouds were long gone; he enjoyed work for the first time in his life and he had no women troubles as such; he was just a sex toy to a hot middle aged women; and he loved it.

Nichola Jones announced that she was expecting her second child; something that made Mack raise his eyebrow and Nichola giggle. It had been a long time since Nichola and Mack had danced the fandango; but it was nice for them to share a giggle and there was more news; Carly had a little girl.

Mack's mam had told him she had seen her dad when she had been at the Metrocentre and he had shared his news with her. Mother and baby were doing well and they had called her January. Mack felt a little twinge of sadness; it should have been him. His face must have shown his disappointment and hurt because Paula was quick to say that they would never have lasted. Him and Carly. They had always been better as friends than as a couple. His mam was right; but still, it take make him wonder if there would ever be anyone who would be mother to his baby!

It certainly wouldn't be Stacey's Mom!

But the game rolled on and he continued to play.

(96) Church   #coldplay

Easter arrived and with it Marty's children's baptism.

There had been some sort of practice before the event; but Mack hadn't been able to make it; work was so very busy. The light nights brought longer working hours and Mack was still busy building his bonuses so would stay at the garage as long as he could.

Marty hadn't been happy; there were things that Mack needed to know for the big day; but he had promised faithfully that he would arrive at the Church early on the day and he would speak to whoever it was to learn about what he needed to do and what he would need to do in the future with regard to Godfather duties.

There was no word from Melissa. Mack knew from his Facebook feed that she had jetted out to Florida with her family; there was the obligatory airport bar shots showing her holding a pint of cider surrounded by her family. A little pang of sadness shot through Mack; she really was lovely and she looked stunning! But what would it have been like if she had still been in his life. He would be forever dumping her and avoiding her because Stacey's Mom had sent him one of her little texts.

No Melissa was better off with the Gods.

The day of the Christening arrived and Mack was as good as his word and arrived at the Church way before he was due to be there.

The Vicar seemed to be expecting him and went through everything that would be happening that morning. He spoke of his responsibility to Reggie in the future; leading a good example; being there for guidance for Reggie. It was all very serious and Mack felt a bit of a shit thinking about what sort of example he could be as a moral guidance for Reggie;

it had been less that 48 hours since he had been a 'text' booty call. It made him feel a little hot under the collar; he had no idea what the Vicar standing in front of him was capable of. Could he read minds?

He was saved from the Vicars scrutiny by a commotion at the back of the Church with the arrival of Marty, Dina, the kids and an abundance of guests.

Marty smiled a huge smile at Mack when he saw him; he really must have thought that his childhood friend wouldn't turn up to take up his Godfather duties. A few minutes later kissed and cuddled; Mack found himself sitting next to Mini in a pew.

Mini; a guilty secret from long long ago. Marty's baby sister who had hero worshipped her brother's friend for years until one night when she was about 18 the inevitable had happened and Mini and Mack had done the deadly deal. It had only happened the once and no one had ever found out about it. But they had remained friends; with depth and when Marty had been ill after the death of one of his work colleagues; it had been Mack and Mini that had been there for him. Together!

She had been off travelling the world and by the look of her tan she hadn't been back long. Mack tried to talk to her in whispered tones but she couldn't hear what he was saying; her ears were blocked she gestured which affirmed that she may had only just flown in; but he would catch up with her later and see what she had been up to. Mack really liked her; she was like the baby sister that he never had; with an odd benefit.

Sitting in the Church; Mack took note of Mini's legs, they were toned and tanned and Mack thought about his own toned and tanned body and whenever he thought about his tan; he pictured the sunbed shop and Stacey's Mom.

It was a mad situation.

She 'text' and he ran. He had gone beyond being putty and now resembled a butter pat that had been left out of the fridge too long and was soft and pliable. She was like somesort of goddess to him. Older; in charge and extremely sexy; she was the biggest thrill of his life.

Mack loved the uncertainly of the situation. He could never be sure that she would ever 'text'. He would wonder if the last time would actually be the last time and he didn't know how he felt about that. She was obviously not relationship material; she was at least twice his age and he was certain that Stacey's dad was in the background somewhere. But he asked no questions; they barely spoke beyond dirty talk, but still. There was no future with Stacey's Mom; it was very much here and now. For now anyway.

The service started and Mack, Mini and some other women who Dina's cousin or something found themselves standing with Marty and Dina and little Reggie as the vicar poured water on his head and they affirmed that they would basically be good people to Reggie.

Back in the pew Mini was smiling at him. They had another common cause. They had been Marty's rocks and now they would be Reggie's.

Another group of people gather around the font. This time is was baby Belle's turn. Baby Bell Mack chucked to himself.

The little service started and Mack watched as the vicar poured water and the baby's head and she let out an almighty hollah that seemed to reach the highest rafters of the Church.

Mack stared; blinked and stared again.

It couldn't be??? How could it be?? But it was.

Around the font stood Dina and Marty. Marty's cousin Naomi who Mack hadn't seen for a million years and to be honest had sort of grown in to her looks because when she was younger she used to look like Jimmy Greaves; a bloke who Mack thought was a workmate of Marty; he thought he may even be his boss but couldn't be sure.

And Elle Pearson!!! What the fuck!! What was she doing there!

(97) Memories #maroon5

The little party around the font made their way back to their seats. Elle Pearson didn't even give Mack eye contact!!

Considering that the last time that he had seen her they had shared breakfast after L Pearson Car's Christmas Party; he was smarted by her aloofness. And very turned on, which was very inappropriate considering he was in Church and he still wasn't sure what the Vicar was capable of with regards to seeing into his soul.

Then the service was over and Mini was whispering in his ear that she really needed a drink; Mack couldn't agree more. But there were photographs to be taken.

Reggie and his Godparents.

Belle and her Godparents.

Reggie and Belle together with their Godparents.

Reggie with each of his Godparents.

Belle with each of her Godparents.

Family.

Extended family.

Friends.

Group photographs.

The photographs went on and on until eventually someone shouted that it was time to go to the pub and Mack found himself back in his car and Mini in the passenger seat.

It was nice to have a catch up. She had been all over the place; was loving travelling the world; she would arrive somewhere; get herself a little job in a bar or something, see the sights and then move on. It was a nomadic life she said, but it suited her she had said. She wanted to write; she had a degree in English Literature but felt she had nothing to write about; her travels were helping and she had the bones for a book.

Mack was impressed. He didn't know anyone who had thought about writing a book and he would certainly have a read he told her when it was published. He would try anyway; he didn't think he had read a book since he was at school; he was a movie man; more recently a box-setter with the arrival of Netflix. But he would at least give it a go.

They had agreed that Marty was a different man. It could have been so different; he really was in a bad place. But look at him now; a happily coupled father of two. They had both laughed as they pulled up outside the pub; there was hope for them two if Marty could do it.

Mack had missed Mini. Before the incident they had always been close. But after they had slept together they had drifted and had barely spoken. It wasn't until Marty had started tail spinning did they get back to some level of communication. Mack made a silent promise to himself that he would keep Mini in his radar in the future; even just a text now and again checking that she was ok; nothing more sinister than that. That ship had well and truly sailed.

In the meantime he had Elle Pearson to worry about. How had she ended up being Belle's Godmother and how hadn't he known that there was a connection between them.

A couple of hours later, Mack was tiddly.

The drink had flowed and even though Mack had half promised himself that he would just drink Coke; with the close proximity of Elle Pearson that idea had flown well and truly out of the window.

Luckily he had already told work he may not have been in the next day. It was a Bank Holiday and he wasn't rostered in, but had sort have half said he may be in. He doubted that he would though; he had already had a pint or three and the day was still young.

His mam and Tom were both there. Marty had been Mack's friend since they were in primary school; Mack's house had been Marty's too and Paula had always had a soft spot for Marty so it as fitting that she would be there on such an important day. And of course Tom too; he was almost family himself soon and Paula had invited Marty and Dina to the wedding.

Mack was sitting with his mam and Tom when Elle Pearson made her way over and sat in one of the empty chair.

As ever; she looked amazing. She was wearing a dusky pink dress; Mack was no fashion officiado but it looked expensive and it suited her just fine. She really was a fine looking girl; especially when she was smiling like she was then at Paula and Tom. All Mack got was a curt nod of the head.

Mack introduced Elle to his mam and Tom; this was 'Elle, Len Pearson's daughter!' Paula then went off at a million miles an hour; just as she did with everyone Mack introduced her to. She wasn't nosy; more interested.

Mack found out more in the next 10 minutes about Elle Pearson than he had in the 10 months or so since he had first encountered her. The interview that wasn't an interview and more a casting couch scenario for some porn movie.

Twitch twitch went his boxer shorts.

It really wasn't the time or the place; but looking at Elle it was like she could read his mind and a smirk crossed her face!

Fond memories.

Anyhow Elle worked in marketing or something; she was divorced; no kids and at that time was happily single.

Then there was that smirk again.

Paula and Elle were getting on like a house on fire. Paula kept bringing Mack into the conversation and Mack kept on sipping his pint and looking for an exit route. As lovely as Elle Pearson was; Mack thought her sitting chit chatting with her mam and Tom was too close for comfort. Mack could hear Paula telling Elle about the wedding in Cyprus; asking about Elle about the dress she was wearing and how something like that would be perfect and then the pair of them seemed to be exchanging mobile numbers; what was that about??

Mack went to the bar; Mini was there and he was on safe ground. As they chatted Marty came across and joined them. The days of Mini constantly rubbing Marty up the long way were way gone; now they had a lovely relationship; Marty went out of his way to make sure Mini got updates with regards to the kids.

Mack was about to ask Marty how he knew Elle when his mam and Tom came up to the bar and Marty was lost to them.

On the table they had vacated; Elle sat looking at her mobile. Mack had no option but to go and join her; it would have seemed petty not to. Taking his pint and the glass of wine that he had got for Elle he made his way back over to the table.

(98) She's So Lovely   #scoutingforgirls

Smiling when she saw him and gratefully taking the glass of wine; they spent the first few minutes agreeing how lovely his mam was; what a lucky mam Tom was and how so far it had been a lovely day.

Considering they had once had a moment; they were a little awkward with each other. It was the first time that he had encountered Elle not in a place connected to or surrounded by Pearsons!!! She was out of her comfort zone and Mack felt a little tinge of sadness.

The thing that had happened had been instigated by Elle; it had all been on her terms; her way and she had dismissed him afterwards as if he was a dirty pair of knickers that she kicked off her foot when she was finished with them. Mack had loved it.

Here today she was a normal girl. There was none of the aloofness of the casting couch; there had been none of the know all looks of earlier encounters; here, sitting in a pub where they were both celebrating the accolade of being Godparents; she was very normal. Beautiful; yes. But she was one of his 'it' girls; the type of females that made his heart beat just a little bit faster and the twitch in his boxer shorts thump. Mack didn't see that today and he felt a little bit sad.

Or was it he was so enthralled with Stacey's Mom that some of Elle's allure had diminished??

Mack couldn't be sure.

But she was very beautiful and Mack wasn't going to miss up on the opportunity of spending some time with her.

Elle was Dina's school friend; the equivalent to Mack for Marty.

And that put an age on her. Dina was 7 years older than Marty; Mack knew this for sure. This made Elle Pearson mid-thirties! So that was two mysteries solved; how she was a Godmother and how old she was.

He also found out that Elle; or Eleanor was the child of Len Pearson's thirds marriage to Elle's mam; Lynne.

The marriage Elle had said had been short and sweet. Her dad had been on the up and all his time was spent at the garage or travelling up and down the country buying cars.

After the break-up of marriage number 2; Len had thrown himself into work. Lynn had been his secretary. Then she was his secretary with perks and then when they found out that they were having an almighty perk between them; Len had married her mam.

But it wasn't a marriage built on love. Len continued to treat Lynn like his secretary even when they lived together as husband and wife. By the time Elle arrived Lynn was already fed up. Len would spend night and nights away from their home; there were the other kids from his previous marriages to contend with so even when he was at home; it was never just him.

Elle hadn't even been 2 when her mam decided enough was enough and they moved out and went to live with her Gran.

They had lived there for almost 5 years. Elle would see her dad whenever he had time; but that wasn't a lot and when her mam met and married Elle's step dad Gary; there was little contact until Elle was in her late teens.

Len Pearson may have been an absent parent; but he had always been generous with his children. Elle was educated privately; she had the best education she could possibly have had and that had resulted in a double degree.

Mack was surprised that she revealed so much about her life. More surprised when she got up and went to get them drinks from the bar.

Marty took the opportunity to come across and ask a few poignant questions about how Mack knew Elle. He hadn't made the connection either; even though he knew that Elle's dad owned a gharage!

The bulk of the party were leaving. The kids were getting cranky and they had drinks and nibbles back at theirs for anyone who wanted to pop back. Mack said he would follow on; Paula and Tom had left and they had kindly taken his car back with them so he could walk the short distance to Marty and Dina's and then get a taxi home later on.

Kisses and cuddles done. Elle returned with their drinks and conversation resumed.

When she was at University in York she had met her husband to be.

He came from Nottingham and upon graduation he had secured a job in Newcastle just like Elle had. He had made the move and she had moved into a house with him and all was well. The wedding was a few years later and just like every other Pearson it had been a grand affair; lavish and the pictures had even been in the local papers.

But the cracks had started to appear in the marriage early on. They had been so focused on their degrees and then their new jobs and then the wedding plans that they barely knew each other. It had been a disaster Elle said. It was over before she had even began.

They chatted like away for ages; another round of drinks and then they decided that they best put in an appearance at Dina and Marty's before they ended up too legless to walk there.

This version of Elle was lovely. The smirk still appeared now and again as they spoke; but they made no mention of the interview that wasn't an interview. She was appealing to Mack but not in the way that he thought she would be. She had been in the 'it' camp; but now seemed to have stepped away from all that and was in a class of her own.

Mack really liked her.

They arrived at Marty's just in time to take part in the Easter Egg hunt; Mack had forgotten that it was Easter Sunday and kicked himself for not getting his new Godson an egg; surely he was big enough to eat one. Mack made a mental note that he would have to try better on all of the other celebrations that where a gift would be expected.

It ended up being a good night. Elle was fun; most of the people who hung back when the kids were put to bed were and they ended up having a game of Cards Against Humanity which was brutal and very funny.

Elle suggested they share a taxi home. Mack had no idea where it was going; did she mean she would be coming back to his?? He couldn't remember if he had told her that he was still living at his mams?? The last thing he wanted to do was take classy Elle back to his boyhood room. It may have not had toys strewn all over the floor, but it still have a boy vibe about it. No that wouldn't be happening.

Or did she mean he go back to hers?? Mack wasn't sure if he wanted to do that either. He liked Elle a lot; but he was so fixated on Stacey's

Mom and her demands that he didn't feel the need to dabble somewhere else.

Or did he not want to sleep with Elle because she wasn't an 'it' anymore!!

A confused and drunken Mack was never good.

But as sure as eggs were eggs if Elle was offering herself up on a plate; he would take it. And then where did they go.

No he needed to go home; sleep off the lager and get himself in to work at some point tomorrow!

If he wanted to be taking people back to his mam's when it was his place then he needed to get the décor sorted quickly so it was more him and less his mam.

So making some feeble excuse to Elle; he said that he was going to walk home after he had put her into a taxi.

Mack kissed her goodnight; no tongues or anything; just a nice lip kiss between two drunken people and waved her goodnight.

They had loosely arranged to go for a meal sometime; they had even exchanged mobiles and as Mack set off on his walk home; which he estimated would take him well over an hour; he thought about Elle.

(99) Call Me Maybe   #carlyraejepsen

It wasn't often he got confused over a female. He was either into them or he wasn't.

He was so into Stacey's Mom. Ball deep into her. But it was a hiding to nothing; and how she liked to smack his hide. Just the thought of her smacking his arse made him tingle. It was just sex with her; amazing mind blowing sex.

Even if there wasn't s Stacey's dad; he very much doubted that there would be any type of relationship. He had no idea if she was smart; obviously was quite smart because she owned the sunbed shop; but he didn't know if she had a sense of humour or she had a kind heart. All Mack got was the cold façade face that held all of her sexual prowess. Not exactly relationship material.

As much as he knew that she was no good for him; he could not give her up. He could try to ignore the texts; he could stop using the sunbed shop. There were so many things he could do to stop contact; but he didn't. He liked what they had; he liked being her beck and call boy. He liked the power she had over him. If it was going to stop then it would be something of her making and not his.

The first time he had been involved with her he had been much younger. There were still so many females to be having sex with in the bits in the middle between meeting. He thought nothing of sleeping with someone else. It was easy come and easy go.

But this time it was different.

More was expected of him. He was past the age where girls would just put up with his disappearance the minute he had lost interest in them.

Nowadays they would expect more.

Elle would have expected more and at that time she was a conundrum to him. He thought she was one thing and she clearly wasn't. What she was though was a beauty; good fun and intelligent. She was coupledom material if the truth be known. And he knew that she had the extra edge about her; but unlike Stacey's Mom; it was something that she didn't wear on her sleeve.

The walk did him good. It was late and there weren't many people around even if it was a Bank Holiday.

It had been a good day and he felt privileged to be asked to be Reggie's Godfather. On paper he wasn't the best person for the job. But he would try. He would get all the important gift dates off his mam and he would make sure that he was ready for each event.

The house was ion darkness when he got home. Maybe his mam thought that he wouldn't be back.

But he was glad he did. Elle had drank as much as he did and was quite tiddly; he didn't want to be a drunken fling. He didn't know if he wanted to be anything.

Deciding that he had definitely pondered about himself far too much for one day; he headed up the stairs and into his bedroom.

Yes he had done the right thing not bringing Elle back.

It might not have had the toys, but it definitely had a teenager's edge about it.

He would move into his mam's bedroom after the wedding.....

(100) Hangover   **#taiocruz**

For the following weeks it was all very much same as same as.

Work was busy; Mrs Jones got a bit of a baby bump and Mack's bonus bumped up each month nicely.

The gym was still a constant as was the 'text' which had no pattern or rhythm to it but the moment it arrived Mack would feel a smidgen of comfort. Whatever it was he had with Stacey's Mom was equally as good for both of them.

Each time they met more and more boundaries were pushed. It was always frantic and always over much sooner than Mack would have liked. He would have liked nothing better than to book them into a hotel so they could spend the night together. But how he would even broach that subject was beyond him; aside from sex they didn't really speak.

But she had a spell over him and while he was in the strange relationship; no one else held his interest.

Mack saw on Facebook that Melissa was in a relationship. He didn't look to see who with; when the notification came through he quickly went to her profile and 'unfriended' her. She really was a lovely girl and he was so pleased that the God's had found her someone who deserved her. But still; he didn't want to see it. He really liked her; but her loveliness hadn't been enough and it was silly pretending it was.

Wedding plans were full on at home.

Much to Mack's surprise Paula had got her wedding dress with the help of Elle Pearson.

A brief conversation at Reggie and Belle's Christening had resulted in Elle suggesting a shop to Paula where she thought there would be something appropriate for her. Elle had even picked Paula up and gone along with her; where low and behold she had been right and Paula had bought a dress. Elle had gone again with Paula when the alterations were made and the two had built up some type of relationship where Elle was acting like Paula's wedding planner.

Mack didn't mind.

Paula didn't have a lot of friends.

When he had been growing up it was always she was at work or she was doing stuff with Mack. Her friends at the time were in their own relationships and Paula was never a one for playing gooseberry. So 'girl' friends had never been something didn't have a lot of and it was nice that Paula and Elle were getting friendly.

Paula said Elle knew a lot of people through her work; the shop where she had bought her dress from had been marketed by Elle and the company she worked for. Elle had even managed to wangle a discount off the manager.

Elle was helping organise a little hen party for Paula; just some spa day somewhere, but Paula's sister in law Lynne was going as well as a few people she worked with; Paula would never have done anything like that off her own back.

Unlike Craig who was all out organising his 'hag party!'

There were 30 of them going to Benidorm for two nights and this included the whole sales team less John Rippon who said he would stay and man the fort with Len Pearson who had agreed to half the garage being missing for a weekend and half of a working day.

Mack, Kevin and Justin were sharing a room and he knew a couple of the mechanics were going but beyond that he had no idea what he was letting himself in for. But Mack was always up for a few days in the sun and when they all met up at Newcastle airport bar before their flight; it was a very mixed bunch.

If Mack had been expecting the majority of the party being made up of Craig's camp mates; he was sadly mistaken; the majority of the blokes there were middle aged and made up of Craig's relatives; their friends and the staff of Len Pearson Cars.

Craig's better half had been banished from the event; he was having his own allegedly on the same weekend but instead of flying off into the sun; he and his mates were off to Amsterdam on the boat.

As much as Craig bigged up his flamboyant side; the group that boarded the aeroplane for Benidorm was a very similar group of males to any other stag do that Mack had been on. They all drank lots of beer in the airport bar; drank more on the plane and then spent the majority of the flight travelling backwards and forwards to the toilet.

But it was a very sombre group that made the return journey a couple of days later.

There was no drinking being done that day. The staff from Len Pearson Cars were all going to have to make their way straight in to work from the airport; but it was a bit of a blessing in disguise and Mack for one was pleased his liver was getting a break.

It had been a mint weekend though. Lots of drink and lots of laughter and more drink and some sunshine and then more drink. Poor Kevin hadn't even made it out the second night; the second day of drinking around the pool had finished him off and he had taken to his bed and had only just got up in time to pack his few belongings and catch the shuttle bus to the airport.

As the first 'Hag' party Mack had attended; it had been a hoot.

Work was a never ending day; it was never going to be ideal coming off a plane and straight into work; but added to that the amount of alcohol drunk; the lack of sleep and the fact that even though John Rippon and Len Pearson had done a sterling job keeping the sales rolling; they hadn't actually done anything and each of the 'hag' salesman had a mountain of paperwork waiting for them.

Mack was so worn out at the end of his working day that he didn't even go to the gym. The only thing he wanted to do was go home; have a shower and sleep.

(101) She's the One   **#robbiewilliams**

There had been a 'text' when he had been in Benidorm.

It had arrived on the Friday evening; as always it just said the time.

Mack was already 3 sheets to the wind by that time; he saw the message and was about to text back when he remembered he had never ever text her back before. He wasn't sure telling her that he was out of the country would scupper any future dalliance.

So as tempting as it was; especially with all the dutch courage throwing through his veins; Mack put his mobile in his pocket and got on with his night.

There had been no more texts.

There were no more text for at least three weeks.

Mack felt quite sad about it; he was kicking himself for not letting her know that he was away and even though he went to her sunbed shop at least three times a week in the weeks following; there had been no sign of her.

It was a barren time.

Mack always seemed to have someone on the go. But Melissa had gone off in the lap of the God's and Becky; his step sister to very soon be had seemed to have put up a wall between them; they were still friendly but any hope that Mack might have had regarding the bopping up and down of her pixie head and seeing her piercings again seemed like an impossibility. But every cloud had a silver lining and even though he wasn't getting up and personal with her; there was always the bonus of match tickets.

Elle was still about; Mack hadn't seen her and the conversation about going out for a meal together had never come in to fruition; but Paula talked about her and Mack knew for a fact that they had met up.

It was funny because Mack had always thought that Elle was someone who would get him. He had fantasied over her plenty of times; the interview that wasn't an interview would always be a feature in his wank bank. But getting to know her; he felt that Elle had taken a opportunity rather than it being her thing. The high heels and the smirk on her face she always wore was a bit of a red herring and to be honest Mack was pleased that he got to know her better before he got to know her better better, he had a feeling that she may be quite a needy girl underneath all of her bravado.

She was no Stacey's Mom!

And that was where Mack's problem lay. No one was Stacey's Mom! She was 'it'. She was the one that got his blood pumping and beyond her there was nothing and no one for him.

With the absence of her from his life Mack once again began to question himself. And he hated himself for doing it.

He had never been short of female attention. He knew that he could turn it on and off like a tap. He turned it on daily when dealing with customers at work, but he also knew that he was changing.

He had done the coupledom thing; firstly with Carly and look what had happened there; then again it had been almost coupledom with Melissa and that had in truth never been anywhere near; he couldn't even begin to think about being faithful to her.

But in some bizarre twist of fate; he was being faithful to Stacey's Mom. She had managed to cast some sort of spell over him and although there was little hope of anything beyond what it was; maybe what it was was all he needed.

Maybe a partner and 2.4 children was never going to be him. It should have made him sad but in truth it didn't.

Very soon he was going to have his mam's house all to himself. His savings were growing and he was looking forward to making his childhood home his house. Beyond Stacey's Mom pumping the blood through his veins; the thought of a place of his own was making his heart race. He had never lived on his own before; there had always been his mam and then there had been Carly and apart from the odd night here and there; there had never just been him.

It was going to be his house; his own space and his haven. Maybe then he would find out who he was and what he wanted to be.

And then the 'text' came and his life felt like it was back on an even keel again.

As ever after work he took himself off to the gym; showered and then made for the sunbed shop where he had himself a 12 minute session and then headed for the treatment room.

(102) All by Myself   #celinedion

The look on Stacey's Mom's face was hard to read; was she annoyed with him. But she indicated that she wanted him naked and she wanted him on the treatment table. Fully dressed she circled the table devouring him with her eyes; she had done that many times; he would be butt naked and she would be fully dressed; but there would always be something tasty hidden beneath her every day wear just waiting to come out.

He was excited. That was apparent. To be honest he had been excited all day; since the text had arrived he had been twitching in his boxer shorts; he really hadn't been sure if he would see her again.

But here he was and even when she started tying him to the treatment bed she wasn't surprised; they had been there before. He liked it. The blindfold was a new thing; as was the gag; but he was up for it; he was up to anything she wanted.

Mack was lying all tied up on the treatment bed; the blindfold was over his eyes and there was a gag in his mouth.

He waited and he waited to see what Stacey's Mom would do next!

He had no idea how long he waited before he realised that Stacey's Mom was no longer in the room.

Then the penny dropped.

This was payback for not turning up after the 'text' weeks earlier.

Mack should have been angry; but he wasn't. He liked it!

For what seemed like an eternity he lay there. He had a hard on that came and went; he had no idea where this was all going and the thought of what was going to happen had his in a right old state with himself.

He could smell her; she came back.

The gag was removed and then the blindfold and when his eyes readjusted he saw that she was still in the same clothes that she had been wearing when he had first arrived. What ever she was wearing underneath hadn't surfaced and Mack had the distinct feeling that they wouldn't be.

Surely she could see how excited he was to see her??

She unfastened him from the treatment bed and told him to get dressed.

Mack did as he was told.

Dressed he made his way outside the shop and waited for Stacey's Mom to make the shop secure; turn on her very high heels and trip trot away from him.

Mack looked at his watch; it was way after midnight. He had been tied up for over two hours.

It was the ultimate revenge.

By the time Mack made it home and into his bed he thought he was actually going to have a mishap in his boxer shorts he was so turned on.

It took a long time for Mack to get to sleep. Just as he thought he had finished he would be twitching and it would happen all over again. Stacey's Mom was the ultimate form of Viagra.

It was all so intense he thought that he may have to ignore another 'text',

But then this time might have been the only time he was given a second chance. That was if this was a second chance anyway …..

(103) Sound of Silence   #simonandgarfunkel

Workwise Mack was in his element.

He had learned so much and was now very much part of the team.

There was nothing he didn't like about his working day; even the mountains of paperwork seemed much more mole hill than mammoth nowadays and he had learned if he kept on top of it; it wasn't so much of a chore.

Mack and Mrs Jones were as close as ever and she laughed when she told him about what Stacey's Mom had done to him. Thought she might try that on Mr Jones if he stepped out of line; Mack doubted it. Nichola Jones wouldn't have the will power.

Mrs Jones would be a miss when she went on her maternity leave; she intended to have as much time off as she could this time; Mr Jones was working so she was going to make the most of the time off. But still; Mack would miss their little coffee break chats. She really was a nice woman.

The weeks ticked by and there was no news from Stacey's Mom.

If that was it, then she had certainly left Mack with an unforgettable parting shot.

The gym was still a constant as was the regular sunbed sessions; and just like last time there was no sign of Stacey's Mom.

There was no time to worry about it though; he had a two week holiday on the horizon and he was exceptionally busy at work.

His mobile was forever pinging; at first he was always eager to see if it was the 'text', but it never was; it would be his mam asking him to call and pick something up on his way back from work; or his Granddad sending him pictures of shirts and stuff from Marks and Spencers and asking if he thought that would do for Cyprus.

So when the 'text' did come; it felt like it was out of the blue.

It was a 'text' but a different one.

This one had a time and a date, a place and what to take.

There was a change in the tempo.

This time it was a Saturday night; it was a city centre hotel and it was a room number.

This 'text' was a game changer.

This 'text' made Mack a little bit nervous and a whole heap excited. It gave him an extra spring in his step and for the days running up to the Saturday night; the world was a beautiful place. The cars sold; the wedding arrangements bounded along to the extent that he had even started packing and he hadn't even minded taking his granddad to the Metrocentre to get all his bits and bobs for the wedding.

Abd then it was Saturday and Mack found himself in a hotel lobby waiting for a lift to take him to the room number that had been on the 'text'

He thought that he looked good; he had finished work on time and went straight home and got himself ready.

He was full of nervous energy.

(104) Hotel Room Service   #pitbull

The Housemartins 'Happy Hour' played on repeat all the way into the City Centre; a song he hadn't listed to since his truck days; he found a parking spot; paid for the longest availability and made his way to the hotel.

Now; waiting to go up to the room; the nerves were replaced by excitement; whatever Stacey's Mom had in mind; she had gone to a lot of effort. She had not just booked a hotel room but had wangled the room number out of them before she had even checked in. Mack had never known a room number until he arrived; Stacey's Mom knew days and days in advance.

His knock on the door was opened within minutes.

And there she was; the smell of Chanel was all over her.

It was all a bit strange. There were no clipped tones telling him to do anything; this time there was a smile and her beckoning him into the room. This was the real Stacey's Mom.

She looked stunning.

Mack's heart was beating so loudly he was sure she would be able to hear it.

In the room the little table was set for 2 and there was a bottle of wine chilling in a bucket.

This was a date night!

Mack was so far out of his comfort zone with her; he felt awkward.

Gesturing to him to take a seat; she asked him if he wanted to pour them some while she answered the knock on the door.

It was room service and as the waiter busied himself placing food on the table; Mack took the opportunity to take in Stacey's Mom.

She really did look amazing.

She was wearing a black dress; classy not too low cut and not too short; it hugged her body perfectly and she was wearing her signature killer heels which gave Mack movement in his boxer shorts.

The waiter left and Mack found himself sitting opposite his ultimate 'it' girl; or in Stacey's Mom's case; woman!

In truth Mack hadn't been expecting a night as normal as it turned out.

Stacey's Mom started off by saying that she felt like she needed to make it up to Mack for how she had treated him last time. Mack said she hadn't need to; he had loved it. But still he did appreciate her going to so much effort.

It was like a regular date.

(105) Heather   #conangray

Her name was Heather; Stacey's Mom had a first name. Heather! Mack had never known that. She had asked for Mack's; had he always been Mack; of course he hadn't but he didn't tell her. The amount of people that knew he had another name was small beyond his family. It even said Mack on his passport; his mam had done it at the same time that she had changed his name from Shearer when he was just a little boy. But his birth certificate said something different altogether!

The ate and they drank and they talked.

Heather was actually single. Had been for a number of years. The sunbed shop where they met was one of 6 that she owned and ran along with a couple of hairdressing shops and a barber's which she was in the process of expanding. She certainly wasn't who he thought she was; she was a savvy business woman.

When her marriage had broken up she had left the business that she and Stacey's dad had ran between them. He had allegedly paid her well and she had invested the money in new smaller businesses and the rest she said was history. Women's and men's grooming was something that something that had always interested her she said.

Then she gave Mack that look!

The food was eaten and another bottle of wine opened and they continued to talk.

It was definitely a date.

Mack told her all about his job at Len Pearson Cars; about his home life and the impending trip to Cyprus to see his mam marry Tom. Mack even told Heather the date; he didn't want to miss another 'text' even. though it had turned out okay the last time. He had loved the treatment. bed and he was loving the night he was having.

But still.

Heather had laughed and said that the date was duly noted.

Excusing herself; Heather made for the bathroom. Mack had no idea if he was staying the night or not; the only thing she had told him to bring with him was a toothbrush which he had done and left in his jacket pocket.

Mack sipped on his wine and took in the room.

The hotel was one of the nicer ones in the city centre; it wouldn't have been cheap. Neither would the food and wine have been. He would offer to go Dutch; Heather couldn't be expected to pay for it all.

Heather??

It was strange calling Stacey's Mom Heather. It was like at school when you called a teacher Miss or Sir and then when you found out their Christian name it would always sound alien and it took a while for them to suit them. It would take a long time for Mack to call Stacey's Mom Heather; Stacey's Mom may forever be Stacey's Mom.

Mack was beginning to wonder if there was something wrong in the bathroom; Heather had been in there a very long time.

Just about to go an investigate; the bathroom door opened and there stood Stacey's Mom as he knew her.

Clad in black laytex; she was wearing the tightest of corsets; stocking; thigh high boots with those killer heels. She had pulled her hair back into a tight pony tail and she had put on some bright red lipstick!

The look on her face was hard and serious and when she ordered Mack to strip; he obeyed.

It was maybe the best night of Mack's life.

Stacey's Mom pressed all of the right buttons.

It was a rollercoaster of thrills; Mack had never had a night like it.

Somewhere during the night and as corny as it sounded even just saying it in his own head; Mack knew that Stacey's Mom or Heather or what ever it was she wanted to call herself was the Ying to his Yang and he loved her for it.

She was 'it'!

It was starting to get light by the time the pair of them staggered into the bathroom and into the shower together.

Mack was a little bit battered and a little bit bruised, but he had loved every second of their night together.

In normal circumstances he would have been having sex with a female that he was sharing a shower with; but the truth be known; he was empty.

He had lost count of the times that he had reached the point of no return.

Heather stood in of him; the red lipstick had gone and her hair was loose and tumbling over her shoulders; she actually looked girlish and nothing like the age that Mack guessed her to be; which in reality had to be about 20 odd years older than he was.

She could have been 40 years older than him and he wouldn't have felt any different.

For the first time in his life; he was with a woman who actually got him.

Heather had no agenda; they had talked through the night; they wanted nothing more from each other than what they had.

She had her businesses and didn't really want to be distracted by having a relationship.

Heather also told her sheepishly that she had a grandchild; Stacey's son! Stacey's Mom was a Granny!!

But she was one hot Marmar Mack told her.

Mack had agreed though; he was happy as it was. He wanted none of it to change. He liked the random 'texts' and if she could flip in and out of Heather and her alta ego Stacey's Mom; then that was all he wanted.

They just got each other.

And that was that.

They had their night together; they let each other see who they were, but then they did what they did best and it was all awesome.

And then she did what she always did and disappeared on him.

(106) Mother   #meghantrainor

The weeks leading up to the wedding in Cyprus were devoid of Stacey's Mom and even when Mack stepped up his visits to the sunbed shop in preparation for getting some proper sun on his body; there was no sign of her.

It was fine though. Mack knew that one day she would be back and in the meantime he had plenty to be doing.

Work continued to be busy. Mrs Jones continued to get bigger and bigger and Mack told her all about his little trip into the City Centre with Stacey's Mom; she was the only one that he had told anyone about. He hadn't even told Marty that Stacey's Mom had been an ongoing thing; just that it had happened years ago.

The night before the wedding was surreal.

Paula had been packing her stuff up for weeks and shipping it over to Tom's. All that was left were the that she would be taking to Cyprus and they were all packed in suitcases ready to go to the airport at stupid o'clock in the morning.

The house felt different; even to Mack who barely noticed anything.

It was happy and sad in equal measure. Mack had left before when he had moved in with Carly; but Paula had lived there since Mack was little and even though there was a bright and shiny future ahead of her; Mack could see she was sad.

So Mack did what they had always done when either of them wasn't feeling themselves; he went and got them a takeaway; a huge bottle of full fat coke and put some banging tunes on Paula's stereo which so far hadn't made it into the back of her car and got a new home at Tom's; Mack hoped it wasn't going. It was old but its sound was quality and of all the things that his mam was leaving behind; the stereo would be one he would keep.

It had always just been Mack and his mam. There had been his nan and granddad; but mainly it had just been them two. Mack wouldn't have changed that for anything.

Tom was a lucky man. Paula was glowing in her newly coloured hair and already faint sign of a tan; had she been having sunbeds?? Had she been going to Stacey's Mom's shop?? But it was more than how she looked; if he said so himself she was a good person; she cared about everyone, not just cared but took care. Mack liked the thought of someone taking care of her because Tom would. The future really was bright for her.

And for him.

When they returned from Cyprus he would be coming home to his house.

It was a new beginning for both of them; the Housemartins blasted out of the stereo; Mack packed the last of his holiday stuff and placed his car at the front door.

All that was left to do was wait until his Granddad arrived in the small hours of the morning to take them to the airport; he had insisted.

So for the last time Mack and his mam switched off the lights and headed for their respective bedrooms to get themselves a few hours sleep before they headed off for their new beginnings.

Sleep didn't come easy for Mack and for once it was nothing to do with twitching in his boxer shorts and an ever ending reel in his head of wank bank scenarios.

It was the last night that the two of them would sleep under the same roof; just like they had done for hundreds of nights before that one. End of an era!

Mack felt no shame in the tears that ran down his cheeks ......

(107) My Name Is   **#eminem**

By the time they were all at the departure gate waiting to be boarded onto the plane the tears of the night before were long forgotten.

Mack's granddad had arrived at the scheduled hour and the car had been rammed with the suitcases and all the hand luggage; it was surprising that the car could actually move it was so full.

But they got there and on their arrival Tom and his family were there already. Becky and her little pixie head kissed and cuddled Mack; she really was lovely but she was about to be his step-sister and there seemed to be an unspoken rule between Becky and Mack that the shenanigans they had once enjoyed would be a thing of the past.

Marty and Dina arrived not long after Mack had got there; it had been touch and go whether Dina was going to get because Reggie had caught chicken pox; but her mam and dad had stepped in and taken the kids for the week and Mack was over the moon that his best mate had made it.

Mack's Auntie Lynn and Uncle Peter were there too.

It was going to be a good week.

All the people he loved in one place; well almost all the people he loved.

Mack had an aisle seat on the plane; his granddad sat next to him and Tom's mam had the window seat.

His granddad was nervous; he had never flown before and he was chatting away to Tom's mam about how he had always took driving holidays when his wife had been alive; Mack could hear Tom's mam telling his granddad about cruises and about all the fantastic facilities they had onboard.

Mack rummaged in his bag for his head phones; he loved his granddad but the thought on constant chatter between him and Tom's mam was too much; better to loose himself in some music and maybe have a little nap; he had only managed a couple of hours when he had eventually dried his eyes and settled down for the night.

Flicking his mobile phone on Mack saw that there was a text. Not just any old text but 'a text'.

Feeling a little bit gutted that Stacey's Mom had forgotten that he was going away and that he was once again going to ignore her and the scary consequences of her either forgetting about her forever or the better of scenario of her inflicting some sort of punishment for his tardiness; he opened the message.

There was a time – 08.30 (an hour from then) and the location was Rear of Plane; Left Side Cubicle as you face the rear of the Plane!

Stacey's Mom was on the plane!!

Mack couldn't believe it. It took him all of his resolve not to stand up and look around for her. But he wasn't going to do that; he wasn't going to blow the instructions. He would sit in his seat; listen to music and wait for 08.30 hours!

He would sit in his seat and listen to music with a throbbing in his boxer shorts which he hoped didn't become apparent to the bevvy of little trolley dollies running up and down the cabin serving the passengers.

Mack managed to sit in his seat until 08.28.

He stood and made his way to the rear of the plane and joined the queue to use the toilets.

It took ages and Mack began to get a little bit hot under the colour in case Stacey's Mom got sick of waiting for him and came out.

But the hold up was very much her fault. There was only one toilet door opening and closing. The door on the left stayed very much shut.

Eventually it was his turn and he tapped on the left hand side toilet door.

It opened and there she was looking amazing and smelling of Chanel No.5.

There wasn't much room; it was frantic and it was over in a matter of minutes; they were so desperate for each other.

Afterwards it was Heather that was saying that she hoped he hadn't minded her gate crashing the wedding.

Mack couldn't have been happier; he wouldn't mind spending time with Heather; because if Heather was there then so was Stacey's Mom and there were so many scenarios that could happen during a week in the sun.

Satisfied that neither of them looked like they had just joined the Mile High Club; Heather went to open the door.

'My name!' Mack said. 'My mam changed it when her and my dad split up; before I started school. My name is Shearer. It's Alan Shearer……..!'

A Note From the Author

I hope that you enjoyed reading Mack Book as much as I liked writing it.

He's a bit of a boy!!

And if you did like it; please spread the word; it is so difficult getting books out to the masses when you do it all yourself.

But I have a head full of stories so check out the ones already written and keep an eye out for news ones.

Love Gill xxx

Printed in Great Britain
by Amazon

25648666R00185